MARY'S SECRET

ROSE OF SKIBBEREEN BOOK 7

By John McDonnell

Discover other titles at John McDonnell's Amazon page:
amazon.com/author/johnmcdonnell.

AUTHOR'S NOTE

This book is about Mary Driscoll, a character in my first "Rose Of Skibbereen" novel. Mary was born in Ireland in 1862 and came to America with her friend Rose Sullivan in 1880, seeking a better life. Their lives took different paths, and this is Mary's story. If you have read the previous books in this series, you know what a lively character Mary is. If this is your first experience with the Rose Of Skibbereen story and you like it, there are six more books available on Amazon. Enjoy!

CHAPTER ONE

1936

Who would have thought it would end this way, with me lying in the street and the life running out of me?

It isn't fair, is it? Ah, but there's no use in complaining. Life just keeps moving, like a fast flowing stream, and there's no good in worrying about what's fair or not. I did better when I stopped worrying about all that business.

And it's all in the past, isn't it? But the past comes rushing back at times like this. I hear the priest saying the prayers above me, but his voice is less important than the pictures rushing through my head, and the voices, and the feelings attached to them. It's all so clear to me, like it's happening before my eyes.

It was a good life, even though it turned out so differently than I expected.

I was born in Ireland in 1862, in a little town called Skibbereen, almost at the tip of the southern end of the country, in County Cork. It was a land of great beauty, but great hardship. I remember the mist in the mountains, the glint of the sun on the sea, the green fields, the long rivers running to the sea, but mostly I remember not having enough. Not enough food, not enough clothing, not enough heat to keep out the cold and the damp. Worst of all, though, was not enough respect.

My family, the Driscolls, had an old name in Cork, and there were stories that some of them went to sea and became pirates. Pirates don't give authority its due, you know, and I liked that part about them. Those days were long gone, though, when I was a child. It was hard times for us, like most others that we knew. The Great Famine had ravaged the country fifteen years before, and it was a specter that haunted every family I knew. There were fresh gravestones in the churchyard from people who'd died, and we all knew the field outside of the town that had the mass grave, where scores of poor starved wretches had been thrown because there was no time to give them a proper burial.

In all this world of misery, however, my family was near the bottom. It was an old story: a father who couldn't support his family and fell into the pit of drink, two brothers who'd started down that path all too soon, and a mother who was nearly mad from the grief of losing her only other daughter during the Famine. My friend Rose Sullivan had a mad mother also, worse than mine, truth be told, and we became friends for that reason. Neither had a mother worth the name, and we mothered each other because of it.

From the time I was a small child I wanted to get out. I'd heard stories of this magical place, America, where there were jobs, and money, and people wore fine clothes and had enough to eat. I'd seen girls leave at the age of 18 and come back to visit five or six years later, wearing fancy dresses and looking radiant with health and good fortune. They said they worked in fine houses for rich ladies, and they got to sleep in a bed with a mattress made out of feathers, instead of the moldy straw beds we used.

"We must go, Rose," I said, when we got old enough. "It's our only chance. We must go now, or we'll be stuck in this miserable place forever."

Rose had a stronger feeling for home than me, and she wavered for a time over whether she could leave Skibbereen, but finally she agreed to go. She wanted to send money back to her family, to help them have a better life than she'd had. I had no such desire -- my family by then had dwindled to my brother Conor and my mother, and I had no intention of giving up my chance at freedom just to stay there and take care of my daft mum. I knew it was a horrid thing I was doing, as I said goodbye to her, probably never to see her again, but I felt if I didn't leave I would surely go mad myself.

Rose and I had many adventures, and we found a good position finally with a family called the Lancasters in Philadelphia. I got three square meals a day, and I was able to buy some nice clothes, but it was never enough. I had a hole inside me that was bottomless, it seemed, and I couldn't fill it with the money I was being paid.

So, I started stealing from my employer. It was only small things, you understand, little pieces of jewelry here and there. I started by sneaking in to the grand lady's bedroom and trying her pretty things on -- a necklace here, a ring there, and admiring myself in the mirror. Then one day I kept one of the baubles. It was a ring, and I thought she'd never miss it. I gave it to a man I'd met, an Irishman of ill repute, and he sold it and split the money with me. I told myself it was only the once, I'd never do anything like that again, but soon enough I took another shiny trinket.

It was bound to end badly, and it did. My friend Rose found some pieces I'd hidden in our room, and she told Mrs. Lancaster. Prim Rose, who pursed her lips and told me I'd done something wrong and she had no choice but to report me. I thought she'd be on my side, I thought she'd understand since we were both trying to escape the same Hell, but no, she refused to understand. I hated her after that, and in the years to come my life took a bad turn, which made me hate her more.

CHAPTER TWO

January 1892

Do you remember Applegate's Mary?

Aye, I do. I got my education about men in that place. A big barn of a place it was, near 8th and Vine streets in the Tenderloin district, packed with hundreds of men drinking and fondling the serving girls, of which I was one. It was not a respectable place for a girl to work, and well I knew it, but I had no hope of getting work as a domestic servant ever again, when I couldn't get a good reference from Mrs. Lancaster. There was no decent work to be had, and I'd had to live in a room in the Tenderloin, a place with saloons, brothels, and flophouses on every corner, a world of sinners it was. There was no respectable work in a place like that, and it doesn't take long before you grow tired of starving and you lower your standards about employment. I didn't sell my body like many another girl in my situation, but I came close a few times. I was desperate to find work so I wouldn't have to go back to Ireland in shame, and Applegate's was my saving grace.

Applegate's was a carnival for the senses. It was huge, taking up almost a whole city block, and inside it had a pipe organ, a carousel with carved animals you could ride on, and a huge bar with eight bartenders filling the glasses of the men stacked four deep in front of them. The bartenders were dressed as circus strongmen, the waiters as clowns, and the waitresses, of which I was one, where dressed in tights and short skirts that were scandalous for the time.

There were dozens of booths where a man could drink to his heart's content if he had the money, and where he could enjoy the pleasure of a serving girl's attentions, for a fee. If the man wanted more, there were plenty of rooms upstairs where he could finish his romancing.

I was buxom enough to fill out a serving girl's costume in all the right places, and for a while that's what I was. I served steins of beer to the gents, enduring their pinches and squeezes throughout the night, and often came home with black and blue marks on my thighs and posterior from their attentions. There was no rule that the waitresses had to prostitute themselves, it was up to the girls, and I managed to avoid it for a good long while. I let the fellows have a kiss or two, or a feel, and that was it. In a year or so, I became a sort of manager of the waitresses, and I was free of the need to walk among the clientele and have my body groped.

Applegate's advertised itself as a circus, a family place, but it wasn't that at all. The men came there to get away from their families, if anything. The owner paid off everyone almost up to the mayor's office, and so it was only raided once in a blue moon, just to keep the respectable folks happy.

It was after one of those police raids that I had my fateful meeting with Peter Morley, Rose's new husband.

It was a bitter cold night in January, and an army of police descended on us, marching the customers and working girls out to the waiting Paddy wagons. I remember one big Irish policeman shoving me into the back of the Paddy wagon with the other girls. He had his hand on my hip, and I pushed it away.

"That's enough from you, Thomas Dolan," I said. "There's no need to be runnin' yer paws over me like that. I'll get in the wagon soon enough."

7

"I haven't got all night, Mary," he groused. "It's cold I am, rounding up all you precious flowers of womanhood on a night like this, and I want to get back to the station and warm me feet."

"You should be ashamed of yourself anyway," I joked. "Applegate's is a fine, upstanding establishment, and there's no reason to upset the clientele this way." I got in the back of the wagon and sat down on one of the wooden benches, pushing one of the girls over with my substantial bottom.

"It's not my idea, Mary, you can be sure of that," Dolan said. "It's just the Mayor's trying to make peace with that damned prissy John Wanamaker, the storekeeper, who keeps stirring up the good churchgoing folks about all the sins being committed at your place of business." He clapped the door shut and went around to the front of the wagon, and in a moment the horses started pulling it through the darkened streets.

"What am I going to do?" the rosy-cheeked girl next to me wailed. "I'm a good girl from a farm upstate. I never should have come to Philadelphia. I never should have gone in that unholy Applegate's in the first place! My parents will disown me. They think I'm going to finishing school at Miss Pennyworth's on Chestnut Street."

"Miss Pennyworth doesn't pay as well as Applegate," I said. "At least, not if you dress in a skirt that stops at your knees."

The rest of the women brayed like donkeys, while the girl pulled the blanket around her that the police had given us to cover our bare legs.

"I was only trying to make a few extra dollars," the girl whined. "Times are hard."

"That they are," I said. "But at least you can go back to your parents, darlin'. I can't go back to Ireland. There's nothing there for me even if I wanted to go."

And well I knew what my reception would be if I ever did go back. By now the news would have traveled through the Irish community in Philadelphia, that Mary Driscoll was a thief, discharged from her position in America because she stole jewelry from the lady of the house she worked in. I was marked forever, and they'd all be turning their noses up at me back home.

For the thousandth time I cursed Rose Sullivan. It was Rose Sullivan who put me in this position, and I hated her with a murderous passion. If I knew a good hex to put on Rose's immortal soul I'd have done it that very night.

The girl next to me sobbed so much I had to give her a handkerchief, which she used to blow her nose loudly. I knew she didn't have to worry about the police doing anything to her or the rest of the girls in the wagon. We'd all spend the night in a jail at 7th and Walnut, but by morning Mr. Applegate would have paid his money to the police to get the charges dismissed, and after a few nights of quiet to satisfy the prudes like John Wanamaker, he'd be back in business again.

Just as I expected, after a fitful night's sleep on a hard bench in a cell, I was wakened by a beefy sergeant who bellowed that we could all go home, our fines had been paid.

"Out of here, the lot of you," he said. "And if you know what's good for you, you'll stay away from Applegate's."

"Oh, I will, sir," the teary-eyed girl from last night said. "I'm going straight back to the farm. You won't see me again."

9

"She'll be back on the job by Friday," said, a buxom red-haired woman named Annie, raising a laugh from the rest of us.

The sergeant shooed us out the door, and we straggled down Walnut Street, looking like Indians with our wild hair and blankets pulled around our shoulders.

I was hungry, and I wanted to eat. I stopped at an outdoor market and bought myself an apple from a man in an apron who spoke with a thick Italian accent, and I went on my merry way eating the apple.

The city was already bustling with life this morning, and I was astonished at all the activity. I worked late at Applegate's and rarely got up before noon, so I didn't know there was so much going on at this hour. The town was bristling with carriages and trolleys, men weaving in and out of them as they crossed the street on their way to work. The grocers and the fishmongers were already displaying their wares, and newsboys were screaming the latest headlines, hawking their papers to passersby.

I glanced up and saw a handsome black carriage going by, pulled by a chestnut horse, its skin already shiny with sweat, and I recognized it as belonging to Mr. Lancaster, the man I had worked for before I was fired. The coachman was none other than Peter Morley.

I looked at his handsome face and felt a wave of anger. This was Rose Sullivan's husband.

Rose, who'd ruined my life.

Rose, who was now married to this man Peter Morley, and had a child with him. Oh, she wasn't working in the grand Lancaster house anymore, prim Rose. I'd heard the whole story from my friends among the Irish girls who worked in the fine houses. Not all of them turned their noses up at me for my crime, and I'd see them at Mass on Sundays, where I'd get all the latest gossip from them. It seems that Peter Morley had gotten Rose with child without the benefit of marriage, and Mrs. Lancaster had discharged Rose immediately. I'd heard she was living in a small boarding house while Peter still worked for the Lancasters.

Something compelled me to follow the coach. I pushed my way through the crowds on the sidewalk, and followed the coach, managing to keep it in sight. Traffic was heavy at this time of the morning, and the horse was not able to move very fast. I saw it turn down Broad Street and head to City Hall, and I followed it all the way to the courtyard outside the building where the carriages were parked. I hung back in the crowd and saw Mr. Lancaster get out, clad in a black business suit and a top hat, and after he said a few words to Peter, he strode briskly into the building.

Peter got down off the front of the coach and tied the horse up at the post and brought a feedbag out and put it on the creature. He was rubbing the horse's back and looking up at the statue of William Penn on top of the building when I walked up.

"You're looking like God's favorite son today," I said.

"And why would I not?" he said, tipping his hat at me. "'Tis a fine day to be alive."

"Do you know me, Peter Morley?" I said, standing with my hands on my hips.

He looked me up and down, taking in my disheveled appearance, without recognizing me. "No. I don't recall meeting any

11

of the Indians they say used to frequent these parts. What tribe are you from?"

"Why, you're as thick as a kettle, man," I said, lowering the blanket so he could see my face better. "It's Mary Driscoll, you oaf. From Skibbereen, and till a few years back working for your same employer. Have I changed that much that you don't recognize me?"

Peter's face broke into a grin. "Why, so it is. Sorry I am that I didn't recognize you, Mary, but you must admit you've changed. Your hair needs a bit more combing, for one thing. It looks like something a bird slept in last night."

"I admit I'm not at my best," I said. "I don't have the money to dress in fine dresses and wear combs in my hair any longer. I can thank your wife for that."

Peter shrugged. "Now, Mary, don't be blaming Rose for your troubles. It wasn't her that stole the jewelry from Mrs. Lancaster, 'twas you."

"And what if I did?" I said. "She wouldn't have missed a few of those baubles. Women like her have so much they can't count it all. None of us gets paid what we're worth, Peter Morley, and I was just trying to set the scales right. And your Rose didn't need to go and report me to the Missus. It was she that was wrong, not me. We Irish are supposed to look after our own, not get a poor girl like me turned out of her job."

He shook his head ruefully. "Well, that's a new way of looking at it. You always did have a novel way of looking at things. But I don't agree, Mary. What you did was wrong."

"I wouldn't be so quick to cast a stone," I said. "I knew you as Sean McCarthy back in Ireland, boyo, and I'd say anyone who comes to America and changes his name like you did is hiding something. There's none of us is perfect in this world, isn't that right?"

A darkness came over his handsome face, and I knew I'd touched a nerve. He seemed to be struggling to hold back some great anger, and I took a step backward, fearing him for a moment. Finally, he mastered himself and said, calmly. "Right you are, Mary Driscoll. There's none perfect in this world."

You weren't perfect, were you, Peter? You were ripe fruit ready to be plucked.

And then it was that I got the idea to make him betray his wedding vows. There was something about that man, a weakness I could sense, that told me he couldn't resist the idea of a woman paying attention to him. I'd had my education about men, working at Applegate's for three years, and I well knew how a man couldn't resist a smile and a wink from a woman.

What of it, I told myself? I was just paying Rose back for the wrong she did me, getting me dismissed from the best job I ever had. Prissy, high-nosed Rose Sullivan, who'd only come to America to feed her starving family back in Ireland, who'd never stoop to such deceit as stealing from her employer! Well, I had no family worth going back to, and I was determined to have a better life than I'd had as a child, and I was damned if I'd go back to that miserable island ever.

So, I turned on what charm I had left after my rough night, and one thing led to another, till just as I thought, Peter Morley was smiling and winking back at me. I had him in the palm of my hand.

13

"Where are you working these days, Mary?" he said. "How are you keeping body and soul together?"

"Why, I work at Applegate's," I said. "I serve beer to the gents, and in return I get a pinch on the bottom, or a kiss sometimes. The pay is good, although I get tired of prying men's fingers off me."

"I've heard about the place," he said, grinning. "It's not an establishment my dear Rose would wish me to go to, I'm sure."

"Well, she won't have to worry for a week or so," I replied. "The bluenoses got the police to raid the place last night, and it's closed. It's why you see me in the state I am. I spent the night on a hard bench in the city jail."

"Sorry I am to hear it, Mary," he said. "I expect it's a hard thing when you can't earn a living."

"That it is," I says. "I don't even have the money for trolley fare to get me back to my room. Would you be able to give me a ride, then?"

He understood in an instant what I was suggesting. "Why, Mary, I don't think Mr. Lancaster would like me driving the likes of you all over town. He's a proper gentleman, and it'd offend his sensibilities if I did that."

"Now that's a fine thing to say to one of your own," I said. "But, I won't hold it against you, Peter Morley. I'll make me own way home, no thanks to you. But if you're ever in the neighborhood of 127 Walnut Street, third floor, number 312, come and ring my bell. I'll be happy to see you, I will. Applegate's will be open again within the week, if I know this city, and I'll be there during the evenings. Stop by any afternoon, though, and you'll find me." I gave him a wink, and he gave me one back.

"I just might do that, Mary," he said. "There are times when His Eminence makes me wait for hours while he's busy with his important legal work. I think I could slip away for an hour and nobody would be the wiser."

"That you could, Sean," I said, using the name he used in Skibbereen. "That you could."

I was just reminding him once again that I knew who he was, and I could see his eyes flash. He seemed about to say something, although he thought better of it, and simply tipped his hat to me.

"I'll be seeing you, Mary," he said.

CHAPTER THREE

It wasn't but a week later that Peter Morley showed up at my door, at 3:00 of an afternoon. I lived in a rooming house with a pack of day laborers, and the place was quiet as a graveyard in the daytime when they were all working, so I knew we wouldn't be disturbed. I was starting back at Applegate's that night, but I had a few hours to kill, and I opened a bottle of whiskey and poured him a drink, sitting at my kitchen table.

"Only one, Mary," he said. "I'm due to pick up Mr. Lancaster in two hours. I mustn't smell of whiskey, or I'll lose me job."

One drink is all I needed to get him loosened up. I went around him and kneaded his back while he sat there, then I ran my fingers through his wavy dark hair, and it wasn't long before we were kissing. I was still young then, and adrift in the world, and maybe I needed the touch of a man to steady me.

Stop lying, Mary. There was no tenderness in what you did.

No there wasn't, I admit. I make no excuses, though. It was wrong, and I knew it, to do what I did. I was trying to hurt Rose, and this was the way I chose to do it.

There was no tenderness, no love involved. It was passion, pure and simple, two people using each other for their own ends. He wanted only a moment of relief from his cares, and I wanted vengeance.

He was a man who knew his way around women, and I'll not say it wasn't a pleasant experience for me in its way. But it was over in the time it takes for a star to streak across the sky, or so it seemed

16

to me. A flash of light, the touch of skin revealed for only an instant, and then he was gone, pulling his pants on and buttoning his shirt, his eyes looking anywhere but at me.

I could see he was wracked with guilt, and so he should, for he'd broken his wedding vows, and him not married more than two years at this point, and a father to boot. It gave me a cold kind of satisfaction to know that I'd gotten back at Rose in this way, even though she didn't know about it.

But I knew, and that was enough.

I went about my business after that with a feeling of justice. It was a bitter justice, though, and I became a little harder inside, lost a bit more of my innocence, because of it.

And then, six weeks later, I found out I was carrying Peter's child.

Of a sudden my bodice seemed tighter, and my serving costume was snug in places it hadn't been before.

"You're stealing food from the kitchen, Mary," said Mr. Pepin, the jumpy little bookkeeper who managed the place for Applegate. He was a small, rabbity man with ginger whiskers and a voice like a squeak. "You've put on weight. You'd better cut it out, or you'll be out of a job. Mr. Applegate's patrons like a girl with meat on her, but not too much."

"I'm just pleasingly plump," I said, laughing it off, but it was a fact that I wasn't feeling well. I could hardly stomach my breakfast most mornings, emptying my stomach when I went to the privy behind the rooming house, and yet I was still gaining weight.

17

It was one of the older girls who set me straight, a girl by the name of Lila. She was the only one older than me, as a matter of fact.

"You're expecting," she said, one night to me, in the kitchen at Applegate's. "Don't you know the signs? I would think at your age you'd know."

"I don't know any such thing," I said. "And I can't be expecting. I'm just not feeling well, that's all."

"That's not what it looks like," she said. "I've seen it often enough. Girls fall for the customers, and they think they're in love. Oh, it's all roses and chocolates for a while. But the passion fades when the men find out they're with child. You should see how fast these upstanding gentlemen run then! And the poor girl is left to clean up the mess. I've helped a number of them deal with it. Who is it, dearie?"

"It's none of these oafs in here," I said. "I wouldn't give them the time of day. They're just here on a toot, but they'll run back to their wives in a minute, and I know that."

"Then who is it?" she said.

"'Tis none of your business," I said. "But if it's true that you've helped others, maybe you can help me. What exactly is available to a woman like me?"

And that was how it started. Lila knew a doctor in Chinatown who could take care of such things, she told me. It would cost me a month's wages, but in the end it would be worth it.

She took me to see him one night a week later after work, and we were the only white people in the area. It was eerie, I won't lie, to be walking those streets at 2 in the morning with no one around. We had to avoid the police, because unattached women didn't go in Chinatown after dark, and it would have attracted suspicion if the cops had seen us. Why, they'd have collared us and taken us out of there for our "safety". It was well known that any single women seen in Chinatown after dark were probably opium addicts or prostitutes, and the police would have suspected us of one or the other.

The doctor's office was down an alley that smelled of cabbage, noodles and onions, and through the back room of a restaurant where Chinese waiters and cooks were playing some kind of card game -- they barely looked up at us as we passed -- and then up two flights of narrow stairs to a filthy apartment where a young Chinese man, barely more than a boy, told me he was a medical student and he could solve my problem for $100.

"We do right now, if you have money," he said, grinning, and rubbing his hands together.

Suddenly I felt sick, and I the room started spinning. I had to get out of there. I ran down the stairs and past the card-playing men, and stumbled out the door to the alley.

"What's the matter with you, woman?" Lila said, when she caught up with me.

"I can't," I said, leaning against a wall to catch my breath. "I can't let him touch me."

Lila didn't understand. "I've taken dozens of girls to him, and only one died, and that was just an accident. He's very good at what he does."

"I can't do it," I repeated. "I just can't go down that path. It's not religion that makes me say that, Lila, it's just something inside me that won't let me do it."

"Well, there's only one other thing," she said, "unless you want to raise that baby yourself. You can sell it."

I had heard of people selling babies, but I didn't know anything about it. Lila filled me in fast.

"There's a place in New Jersey, called a baby farm," she said. "Women go there to have their babies, and they sell them. Some of these rich society women can't make a baby on their own, so they buy them from girls like you, who don't want what's growing inside them."

Do you remember, Mary? How you saw that as a way out?

I had no prospects. I had no skill except keeping house for the fine ladies, but that door was closed to me since my experience at the Lancasters. And I had about one week left before Mr. Pepin showed me the door at Applegate's. I was getting too big for my costume as it was, and they wouldn't tolerate me any bigger.

So what was I to do? It seemed there was no other choice. I packed a suitcase and Lila took me on the ferry and the train to the baby farm, in a place called Merchantville, New Jersey. I spent the next few months working in the kitchen and making baby clothes they could sell to make a few extra dollars.

Peter Morley knew nothing of this, and I wasn't about to tell him. Why would I do that? I wasn't in love with that big oaf, handsome though he was. He was too slippery for a girl to make her life with, I well knew that. I was certain he'd cause a world of pain to Rose Sullivan, that was sure as daybreak. He was a rascal, and would never be true to anyone but himself, and why would I want to be mixed up with someone like that?

I suppose I could have kept the child, but how? I could barely keep my own mouth fed, let alone an infant. A woman without a man in those days had small chance of staying off the streets. I did not want to condemn a child of mine to a life of misery and starvation. Better the child should go off to live in comfort and ease with one of the fine people, and that was that.

It was the better plan, I told myself.

Over and over again, I told it to myself.

It was at the baby farm that I met Angela, an Italian girl who'd gotten in a family way and been sent there by her family to fix the problem. She was a skinny little thing, brown as a berry, who used to cry herself to sleep at night. She barely spoke English, but I took it that she'd brought shame on her family by getting pregnant by a handsome salesman who'd come to their house to sell them an insurance policy.

She had her baby and when they took it from her she screamed like a banshee, and it made all the girls shudder and quake. The man who ran the place, a little German named Mr. Pfeiffer, tried to shush her, but she wouldn't shut up. He finally had her tied up and stuffed a sock in her mouth for the night. In the morning she was gone.

I wasn't going to make that kind of a fuss, I told myself. I was 30 years old, not a girl like that Angela, and I'd been around the block a few times, as they say. I was just dealing with a problem in my life, and I'd be done with it and that would be that. I'd go back to my old life, and I'd be the same old Mary, full of fun, the lass all the men liked for her brassy ways.

But when the day came and I felt the pains coming on, I was weak as water. I cried and screamed just like Angela, and the midwife had the time of it with me. It took hours and hours, it seemed, and when it was done and I heard my baby take its first breath, the tears were coming down my cheeks. I asked the midwife what it was, boy or girl, and she told me it was a boy. I said, "Ah, then God bless him, he'll have a better life than if I'd had a girl."

I asked to hold him for just a moment, and the midwife, a buxom woman with a red face and a stern manner, said, "It's not allowed, Mary, you know that. It does no good -- you'll just make yourself sad."

I pleaded with her. "Have a heart, woman. It may be the only child I can ever call my own. I want to know what it feels like to hold my child in my arms."

She sighed mightily but gave the babe to me, wrapped in a red flannel blanket. I kissed his little face, and he stopped crying and opened his eyes and looked me, staring as if I were the strangest thing he'd ever seen -- as I probably was. His eyes opened wide, taking my measure.

"He's looking at me," I cried. "He knows his mother!"

"Now, Mary, I told you it would do no good," the midwife said. "You're just getting yourself upset. Give him to me, and I'll take him away and let you rest."

"No!" I said. "He's mine, and I want to hold him some more. I want to name him. I'm his mother, and I want to give him a name."

"And what good would that do?" the woman said. "His new parents will give him a name. Whatever name you choose, it won't be his real name."

"It'll be my name for him," I said. "My name, the one I'll call him forever. That will be his real name, not the one the others give him. I'll call him Lucio, that's it. Angela told me it's Italian for light. I can see the light in his eyes, and that's what he'll be to me -- Lucio, or Luke."

And then the most amazing thing happened. When I called him Luke, he smiled. I know you'll say it's just the raving of a crazy woman, to think that a baby just born would smile at its mother. They say babies don't really know they're smiling -- it's just a twitching of their mouths, or maybe a face they make when they have a discomfort in their stomach. But I know he smiled, my Luke -- I know.

I can still feel the ache of emptiness when that midwife took Luke out of my arms. It was like a hole opened up, like my beating heart had been ripped from my chest. I always thought when people said their heart was broken, it was just an expression. Nobody really thinks their heart is broken, I believed. Well, I felt my heart crack and shatter that morning, and I never was able to put it back together, even now, all these years later.

For days and days I didn't get out of bed, and I wouldn't speak nor eat. I just lay there curled up in a ball, and I wanted to die. I was not the Mary Driscoll I'd been up to that point, for in a way that Mary Driscoll had died. Jolly Mary was gone. I had no wish to laugh or tell a joke again; the laughter had gone out of the world for good.

I stayed that way for a long time, maybe a month or more. I don't know how long it was. I was just waiting to die, that was all.

CHAPTER FOUR

And then one morning I just got out of bed, drew myself a bath, fixed my hair and had some breakfast, and decided that I was going to live. I packed my bag, paid my bill and said goodbye to Mr. Pfeiffer and the rest of them, and I took the train to Camden. It was a glorious fall day, and I could smell the river and see the statue of William Penn standing there on top of City Hall, surveying his town and finding it good. I took the ferry over the river and stopped at the market and bought myself a bag of apples, and they tasted sweet when I bit into them. Mr. Pfeiffer had paid me my money for selling Luke, and I had enough to take a room at 4th and Wharton streets, in a houseful of bricklayers, masons, and dockworkers. I told the landlady I'd cook breakfast for them if she'd give me cheap rent, which she did.

It was a quiet life and I liked it, and for a while it suited me. Anyone meeting me would say I was a happy person, but inside I knew there would always be a sadness that never went away. There was no point in dwelling on that, however. I had to move on.

Every night in bed, though, I'd say a prayer for my Luke, hoping he was alive and healthy, and had found favor with God.

It's a funny thing, but I never had much time for the priests and their lot. I don't know if there's a God behind all this business, and if there is one I expect I'll get my punishment fair and square, for justice must be done. But I didn't want anything bad to happen to my Luke, and I couldn't help asking for God to keep him under His wing.

I went along this way for quite a long time, just living day to day, but in time I started to get some of my old fire back. I wasn't all right inside, and there was always that wound inside me, but slowly I felt more like my old self.

And what did my old self want?

Money. It seemed to me that money would cure all my ills. I'd look at all the fine women walking down Market street in their long dresses and their fancy hats, some of them with their servant girls walking behind them carrying the packages they'd bought in all the fancy shops, and I saw how the poor folks had to make way for them, the grimy laboring men tipping their hats as these queenly women walked by. Those men, and people like me too, were invisible to the fine women, nothing more than an insect buzzing around their ears, and they quickly forgot about them.

In 1893, though, it was getting hard to look away from the poor, because there were more of them. Like a storm blowing up on a calm day, the Panic of 1893 came upon us, and almost overnight there was no work, the jobs went away, and men were flocking to the soup kitchens. Of a sudden the house I lived in lost half its boarders, and Mrs. Morgan, the landlady, was making noises about letting me go.

Times were hard, and there was desperation in the air. I didn't want the old familiar ache of hunger to come back, but I didn't know what to do.

I had to find another path. There weren't many opportunities for a woman like me in the 1890s, though, you can be sure of that.

The answer came to me in the form of Aloysius Declan O'Toole. He came to live at the boarding house, and from the first day I saw him, I fell in love with him. He was a mick right off the boat from Dublin, just like so many others, but there was something different about that one, you could tell it as soon as you laid eyes on him.

He was broad-shouldered, with a shock of jet-black hair and blue eyes like deep pools, and bushy black eyebrows. He was quick with a smile and a joke, but there was an edge to him, a sense that it would be a mistake to cross him. He was an intelligent man, that was clear. Even though he was a dockworker, and could talk to the workers in their language, he was also fond of quoting literature, and I'd sometimes see a book of poetry in his back pocket as he went off to work.

I used to sit outside on the steps off the kitchen in the evenings peeling potatoes, and O'Toole started to sit with me. He'd have a smoke, and sometimes he'd help me peel the potatoes.

"Begor, we haven't come far, have we, Mary?" he said, holding up one of the potatoes and examining it like a collector would look at a butterfly. "We're still eating these lumpy things, just like back in the old country. We haven't moved on to steak and truffles, have we?"

"I wouldn't mind a morsel of a nice, juicy steak once in awhile," I said. "I get sick to death of potatoes, although that lot of men inside would eat them day and night if you let them." Suddenly Aloysius tossed the potato down the alley, where it skittered along the cobblestones and bounced off a trashcan.

"What did you do that for?" I said. "You wasted a perfectly good tater."

"Let the rats have it," he said. "It suits them better than me. I have other ideas for my supper."

"Oh, are you going to dine on steak and truffles, are you?" I asked.

"If I bring you a steak, would you cook it for me?" he says. "And be my guest at dinner? I'll happily share it with you."

I laughed. "Aloysius O'Toole, if you bring me a steak I'll cook it, if I don't die of shock first."

"I'll meet you here in two hours, after those lunks have had their supper and they're asleep in their beds," he said. "I'll bring all the fixings for a good meal, and you cook it for me. Then we'll dine like kings!"

"It's a deal," I said. "Although I don't know how you're going to manage it, lad."

"You leave that to me," he said.

The laboring men all went to bed early, because they had to be up and out before dawn, so the night was still young when Aloysius O'Toole showed up in my kitchen with his bounty. He had a thick porterhouse steak, some fresh clams, a box of blueberries and a bottle of red wine, of a good vintage he claimed. You could have knocked me over when he spread this treasure out before me, but he wouldn't tell me where he got it.

I cooked it up and served it to him on a little table in the kitchen, and we whispered as we ate, for we didn't want to waken the other boarders. I didn't have to worry about Mrs. Morgan, the landlady, for she was deaf as a post and nothing woke her short of an anarchist's bomb going off next to her bed.

The steak was like nothing I'd ever tasted; so tender you could have cut it with a spoon, the juices running from it and the flavor like heaven itself. I ate like I was starving, and I was, in a way -- starving for the kind of food like this that the fine people ate. I barely took time to speak as I ate, and every once in awhile I'd look up at Aloysius and see him grinning at me.

"It gives me great pleasure to see how much you enjoy that steak, Mary Driscoll," he said, chuckling. "It's almost more pleasure than the taste of it in my mouth."

When we were finished we sat outside on the steps with our wine, looking up at the full moon through the gap between the buildings all around us.

"It was a fine meal," I said, finally. "But will you not tell me how you came by food like this? I don't suppose you have a secret, do you?"

He smiled. "That I do, Mary Driscoll. But I think you're the type of woman who can be trusted with a secret like that."

"I can keep a secret," I said.

"I thought so," he said. "The fact is, Mary, that I've got this country sized up pretty good, though it's not long I've been here. You know, I was educated by Jesuits in Dublin, and I'm a literate man, but all the classics they taught me gave me wisdom to see through the world's falsehoods. I don't believe in the goodness of Man, not a bit of it. I'm a practical man when it comes to that. I believe that you get ahead in this world by looking out for yourself.

29

You must shift for yourself, for no one else will do it for you. And this is a fine country for a man with my outlook. Why, I could tell that the first week I was here. You look around, and you can see that the grand people are the ones who got here first, and beat everybody else down to get their slice of the pie. They didn't worry about niceties, my girl, not them. They took it by any means necessary, and they gave no quarter. You need look no further than the Indians to know I'm right about that. Where are they now, I'd like to ask? This was their land, just like Ireland was our land, and the newcomers took it away."

"I've never met an Indian," I said, "but I've heard that what you say is true."

"Of course it's true," he said. "I won a blue ribbon in history, darling. I read all the books, even the ones the Church banned. Especially those!" he said, chuckling. "I used to frequent a bookseller in Dublin, an atheist he was, and he had a back room with all the books the Church had on its condemned list. I spent many an hour there reading, and I learned more than the priests ever taught me."

"And what does this have to do with me?" I asked. "I don't need a history lesson from you, Aloysius O'Toole. I'm more wanting to know how you got your hands on this prime piece of meat."

"Ah, that," he said, a twinkle in his eye. "Well, I have a friend who works at the central train yard, where they bring in the cars with all the goods to sell at the stores and the restaurants, for the fine people. He lets me know when there's a shipment arriving, like some prime steaks from the Kansas City meatpacking plants, and I make a visit during the wee hours of the morning, and you might say I borrow a case or two of the contents."

"Borrow?" I said, laughing. "So that's what you call it? I've heard it described with other words."

"So you have," he said, chuckling. "The Jesuits taught me how to split hairs when it comes to ethics, but there's no getting around it -- it's stealing, by any standard. Now, Mary, if that word makes you squeamish, tell me now, and I'll speak no more of these things."

"I've done worse than steal a case of steaks from a train," I said.

"That's my girl," he said. "I thought I had you pegged right. Now, I have a proposition for you. I know you said you'd worked as a maid for a rich family."

"That I did," I said. "But I also told you I lost my position because of a traitor named Rose Sullivan Morley. I took a bauble from the grand dame of the house, and Rose turned me in. I had no prospects after that, for I could get no position without a reference, and so I've lived by my wits these past few years."

"Ah, but you still know girls who work at the fine houses, is that right?" he said.

"I have friends here and there," I answered. "I see them at Mass on Sunday. I've found that going to Mass is the best way to stay up on all the gossip, for we usually sit together and talk. Why do you ask?"

"Because those friends can help us," he said. "My idea is that these girls are a doorway to the rich ladies and their husbands, and we might be able to offer their employers something they'd like, something that would turn a profit for us."

"And what would that be?" I said.

"Why, fine dresses, good foodstuffs, furniture, even. There are lots of fancy items that come to the train yard every day," he said. "And if some of it should find its way into our hands, and then into the houses of the rich and powerful, who's to care?"

"You want me to help you get rid of your stolen goods?" I said.

He laughed again. "Why, Mary, you have a very direct way of putting things. I would call it finding a good home for some of these products."

"And what makes you think the serving girls will take the bait and talk to their employers about these things? If they're caught, they'll be sent back to Ireland."

"Ah, Mary," he said. "People will take that risk if there's something in it for them. If we give these girls some cash, a pretty dress, a piece of jewelry, they'll take the risk. And when the fine ladies get a whiff of this, they'll be all over it, to be sure."

"I don't know," I said. "I'm not as clean as the driven snow, to be sure, and you'll never mistake me for a nun, Aloysius. But I've never been a part of something like this. I stole some jewelry from my employer once, but that is different than what you're proposing."

He put his hand on mine and looked at me with those deep blue eyes. "This is not a time for quibbling," he said. "Have you no eyes in your head? Look around you, Mary. The country is in a panic, brought on by the big European banks, who started to cash in their bonds for the gold this country has stored away. I read the newspapers, girl, and I've been following this for a year now. Did you not see that the Philadelphia and Reading Railroad went into receivership? Why, that's one of the biggest railroad companies in the land, and they're almost bankrupt. The panic is spreading, and in another few months, none of these poor micks who live in this house are going to be able to make a day's wages, and they'll be out on the street. And you'll be right behind them, Mary. It's a hard world, my girl, and we must fend for ourselves any way we can.

I thought it over. "But do you really think the fine ladies will have anything to do with stolen property?" I said.

"Don't worry yourself about that, Mary," he said, chuckling. "I know human nature, girl, and the rich are the ones who would be the most open to this idea. They don't have the same moral code as the poor. If they have a chance to get something of quality at cut rate prices, especially in times like these, they'll take it, you mark my words."

"And what's in it for me?" I said.

"That's the spirit, Mary," he said, slapping the table. "'Look out for yourself first,' that's my motto. There's money in it for you -- you'd get your cut, of course. It's a chance to lift yourself out of this cesspool of poverty here. And of course, you'd have my undying gratitude." He smiled, and his eyes twinkled.

I won't lie; a thrill went through me when he looked at me like that, and spoke to me in the low voice he used when he was trying to be charming. I looked away for a moment, thinking about it.

Then I turned to him and said, "Count me in, Aloysius."

CHAPTER FIVE

You crossed a line, didn't you Mary?

It's true I took those baubles from Mrs. Lancaster, but that was a trifling matter compared to this. You could see just to look at him that Aloysius Declan O'Toole wasn't going to stop at pilfering a few cases of meat from a train car. I knew it wouldn't be long before he'd expanded the operation in a big way.

And I was right. Within a few months, Aloysius was stealing so much from the train yard that he had to rent a small warehouse where he could store his treasures. Before long, we had a brilliant little operation. Aloysius would tell me what he'd lifted from the trains, then I'd put the word out to my friends who worked as serving girls, and they told the coachmen who worked in the fine houses, and I'd meet them at the warehouse where we'd transact our business. Aloysius took care of all the details, including paying off the policemen who patrolled the warehouse district, so nobody bothered us. It was a "mutually satisfactory arrangement," as Aloysius put it.

The money was rolling in, and I had it stored in strongboxes in my room. Banks were closing left and right at that time in 1893, and there was no point in putting the money there. Besides, I liked having the money close to me.

I didn't spend much of the money, not wanting to attract attention to myself, but it gave me a good feeling to know it was there. Sometimes in the evenings I'd go up to my room and open the boxes and spread the money out on my bed, and it did my heart good to see it. Me, Mary Driscoll, the poor girl from Skibbereen, with more money than I'd ever seen before! It was like a dream, don't you know.

But Aloysius was not a man who was satisfied with small successes. He wanted more, and before long he came to me with an idea.

"Why don't we use some of the money to set you up as the proprietress of a little dress shop on Chestnut Street?" he said.

"Now why would I want to do that?" I said.

"Because it's the perfect cover," he explained. "Think of it, Mary. You could offer the kind of dresses that all the serving girls want to wear when they go out to promenade on Sundays with their gentleman friends. You'd have them all flocking to you, and you could easily speak to them about whatever treasures we have to offer that week, perhaps transacting some business in a back room. We'd still have the warehouse, but maybe we could store a few things in the dress shop, and you could give them a look, just to whet their appetites. It's a perfect idea for increasing business, wouldn't you say?"

I had to admit it did sound brilliant. I always had a weakness for fine dresses, and I loved the idea of a shop where I could have the latest styles on display. And it would attract the Irish girls like flies to honey. I knew well how quickly those wide-eyed girls who got off the boat wanted to shed their dowdy clothes and dress like the fine ladies they saw in America.

"What do you say?" he said, a twinkle in his eye. "Will you do it, Mary?"

"I will, Aloysius, you rascal," I said. "Though sometimes I think you're the very Devil himself, how you keep tempting me to do what I know isn't right."

"Ah, Mary," he said, winking at me. "You know I'm only opening the doors to rooms you already want to be in."

He was right, I wasn't being pushed or pulled to do any of it -- it was of my own free will, that's true. But there was another part, I have to admit. I was mad in love with him. The man was like a black-haired whirlwind, and I felt more alive when I was around him. He made me tingle every time he looked at me, and I could live a whole day on one of his mischievous smiles. I wanted desperately to kiss him, but he kept things light and comical all the time, never once acting as if he were interested in me romantically. I was at a fever pitch every minute in his presence, and I wanted so badly to make love to him that it was driving me mad.

So, I had a selfish reason for opening the dress shop with Aloysius -- I thought this would bring him closer to me. In those days women didn't own businesses, so he had to pretend that the shop was his, and that we were married to boot. There was an apartment above the shop, and Aloysius suggested we move in there, since Mrs. Morgan was starting to ask too many questions about some of the people who were showing up at odd hours to talk to me outside the kitchen door. There was no way an unmarried man and woman could live together in those days, though, so Aloysius told the landlord of the apartment above our shop that we were married.

When I heard him say those words my heart leaped, because I thought an arrangement like that would surely bring us together in the same bed.

So it was that we opened a little shop on Chestnut Street, and we lived above it in a three-room apartment. I didn't know a thing about how to buy dresses to stock the shop with, but I learned fast. I had a friend who worked in the John Wanamaker department store, and from her I got the names of some local dressmakers. I called on them and presented myself as Mrs. O'Toole, lately of the United Kingdom, and I was opening a small shop for the fine ladies, and would they care to do business with me? Some of them were a bit flummoxed by a woman business owner, but I knew enough of how the fine people carried themselves that I could bring off a convincing impression of a rich lady, enough to calm their fears.

In a month we were open for business, and I had the place stocked with the very latest fashions. We put up a big sign, and we ran some advertisements in the newspapers. I made sure I went to Sunday Mass wearing my best clothes and a brand new broad-brimmed hat, and afterward I told all the serving girls about my shop. Before long they were stopping by, and when they did I'd take them in the back and show them whatever Aloysius had managed to lay his hands on that week.

Their eyes would get as wide as saucers when I showed them some beautiful dress, modeled on the latest fashions from Europe, and told them the pittance I would take for it. "Wouldn't your missus love this?" I'd say. "I'm sure she'd be happy if you put her wise to a bargain like this. And I'll give you nice cut of the price if you bring her in here and she buys it."

It did not take long before the carriages with the fine ladies were parked outside my little store, and I was ushering those regal madams to the back room and showing them my wares. They all asked where I got such fine goods, and I'd give them a story about how I had connections in the fashion business who found me the best deals, but I knew they didn't believe a word of it. They were too busy running their fingers over the silks and satins and fine linens and imagining what a sight they'd be with that material draped over them.

In a matter of months Aloysius and I were living like royalty, with steak and champagne every night for dinner. When we had the fine ladies hooked, Aloysius expanded our offerings to men's suits, shoes, hats, and that was only the half of his plans. It was amazing to me how his mind worked. He thought of everything. He knew we'd attract attention, and the authorities would start to wonder why we had all these rich people coming through our door, so he paid them off, from the policeman on the beat all the way up the line, to keep them from asking too many questions.

Life was good, wasn't it Mary? But you weren't happy.

It was maddening to me to work so closely with Aloysius but yet not be as close as I wanted. He had affection for me, I knew that, but only as jolly Mary, the good time girl he could laugh and joke with. His partner in crime, you might say.

We shared a bed, but he spent little enough time in it. Many's the night Aloysius wouldn't come home till the sun was peeking in through my window. "My office hours are at night, Mary," he'd say. "I can't be waltzing around the train yard in broad daylight, you know that."

Of course I knew he was right, but it didn't warm me when I woke in the middle of the night and wished for his body next to mine. In the mornings I wanted so badly to stay with him in bed, but when I'd put my arm around him as he crawled under the covers, he'd give me a kiss and say, "Now, Mary, you'd best be getting the

I insisted on one thing, though: I'd never touch or see that foul drug, and I'd have no contact with it whatsoever.

"'Tis not much you're asking, Mary," he said. "I well know the police won't allow it beyond the boundary of Chinatown. There'll be no opium den in the back of this shop, I can promise you that. I've no wish to get on the wrong side of the Philadelphia police force. No, my man in Chinatown will handle all of the dirty work of pipes and beds and the like. You and I are just the middlemen, but for that we get a nice cut of the profits."

"I'll take no cut of that," I said. "It's dirty money, to my mind, and I want none of it."

"Suit yourself," he said, chuckling. "It's more for me, then."

So we started down that path, and many's the day I've regretted it. It started small at first, just a word I slipped to the fancy women here and there, sort of planting the seed in their minds. Aloysius had business cards printed up advertising something called, "The Lady's Remedy", and he had a drawing of a poppy on it. It had no other information on it, save the words, "Inquire of the proprietor," which was me. We had the cards in the store, and when someone would ask about it, I was to size them up before I told them what it was all about. If it was someone I didn't know, I was to go in the back and give them a bottle of patent medicine, some cheap watered-down elixir Aloysius had stolen. He'd taken the labels off and put new ones on the things. I'd give them a bottle and off they'd go with the worthless stuff.

Now, if it was a lady I'd done business with, though, and I knew her to be someone who was looking for a new thrill to distract her from the boredom of her luxury, I'd give her a bottle of stronger stuff. It was pure laudanum, a tincture of opium and alcohol, stronger than anything they could find on the open market. I'd send them off with it, and when they came back a few weeks later, I'd give them another. After three or four trips like this, they'd be looking for something even stronger, and that's when Aloysius got involved.

He'd have a chat with them in the back room, and he'd turn on the charm. Why, he had the perfect solution for them, he'd say. He had a friend, a very learned man, actually, who had a little operation in Chinatown, a shop full of herbal remedies and ancient Chinese notions, a man who could cure whatever ailed them. It was a crime, he'd say, how modern medical science conspired to keep the lid on these time-tested remedies, for fear that the Asiatic race would take over all of our medical industry, if given half a chance. Here was the wisdom of the ages, just a few blocks away, right under our noses, but of course it had to be kept secret lest the legal establishment stamp it out.

He truly had a golden tongue, did Aloysius, and many a time the women would arrange to meet him at the little shop in Chinatown. Usually after that Aloysius was finished with them, for his services were no longer needed. It only took a few trips to the "shop" before they were hooked, and then they'd have found their way to the place in the middle of a blizzard, they had such a hunger.

It was one more scheme Aloysius had to make money, and although it never became his main source of income, there was enough traffic coming through our shop and ending up in Chinatown that he had to increase his payments to the police, to keep us secure. Some of these women had husbands who were powerful men, and if they got wind of what was happening and sent the law down on us, we'd have been in a fix indeed.

Aloysius was smart enough that he took great care to keep the operation secret. He gave me strict orders about who I was to send to him. It was to be society women only, and no more than one or two a month, because any more and it would attract too much attention. And his friend in Chinatown was under orders that these women were not to disappear. Aloysius didn't want them turning up in a brothel in San Francisco or New York, because it would cause a public outcry, and no amount of police payoffs would keep him out of trouble then.

Even though I tried to keep a limit on the number of women I sent to him, it wounded me every time I sent even one. As time went on, I saw them turning from haughty, regal dames who lorded it over me to pale, nervous creatures with a wanting in their eyes that they couldn't fill. I didn't see the end of it, because I lost track of them once they started going to Chinatown, but sometimes I heard stories from the Irish girls who came in my shop.

"Mrs. Cadwell doesn't do much of anything anymore but tell her coachman to take her to Chinatown. Her husband can't do a thing with her."

"My missus went to call on Mrs. Simpson the other day and said she looked a fright. She's lost weight, and she can't seem to concentrate for more than five minutes."

Every comment made me feel terrible, and I could barely sleep at night for thinking about it.

I did my best to get it out of my mind, but then came a time when I couldn't any longer.

I was walking down Market Street one day when I saw a creature come toward me that looked like a ghost. She was dressed in a filthy dress of dirty white muslin, and her hair was wild. She was wraithlike, thin and muttering to herself, with a wild look in her eyes. As I passed her she suddenly grabbed my arm, and said, "Have you a few pennies, lady? I'm sick, and I need to get some medicine."

With a shock that went all the way to my toes I recognized her. She had been a grand lady and debutante named Alice Penforth, and when I first met her she lorded it over me like she was the daughter of the Queen of England. A spoiled rich girl if ever there was one. She had a turned up nose and skin like alabaster, hair like golden silk piled high in the latest style. Now she looked like a harridan, a wasted creature living on the edge of a cliff and ready to fall off at any moment. I saw Death in her eyes, and I knew it was only a matter of time before she was gone. I reached in my purse and gave her everything I had, probably a hundred dollars in coins and paper money, and she looked at me like I was her savior.

"Thank you," she said, with tears in her eyes. "Thank you, kind lady." She embraced me, and I could feel her bony ribs through my corset. Then she ran off, to get herself a pipe, surely, and I leaned against a building to keep from fainting.

You're to blame, Mary, I said to myself. You've killed that woman as sure as if you'd shot her with a gun.

That's when I knew I had to get away from Aloysius.

CHAPTER SEVEN

I've never claimed to be pure as the driven snow, and anyone who knows Mary Driscoll knows there's little similarity between myself and a nun. I'm a practical woman, and I know how the world works. You get along in whatever way you can, and don't fret about the niceties. The priests have time for that, with their fine robes and their rectories with their servants, but a common sort like me can't worry about those things. I never worried about the right or wrong of my actions, and I hadn't been to Confession in many a year.

But there came a time when I couldn't look myself in the mirror, what with the things Aloysius had me doing. The ladies with their opium habits were just the last straw, but it had been itching at me for quite a while. Aloysius kept expanding his operation, and in time he'd gotten mixed up with some very bad characters. There was an Irish gang called the Schuykill Rangers, and a nasty lot they were. They robbed and stole, and they weren't above murder when it suited their purposes. Aloysius used them as muscle when someone crossed him.

He'd started a cockfighting operation in an abandoned warehouse by the river, and he was getting a good crowd who came to drink and bet their money. He'd lend them money, too, when they needed it, but at rates you'd never see a bank charging. If they couldn't pay him back, he used the Rangers to beat it out of them.

I kept trying to ignore the dirtier parts of the business, but it was getting harder to do so. Aloysius was away more than he was home, and sometimes he'd have meetings in the back room of the shop with a shady character or two. I didn't like the look of these men, and I told him so.

"They have their purpose," he'd say. "Everyone has their bit of usefulness, Mary. That's how it works."

"What use can men like that be to you?" I said. "They're a bad lot, I can tell just by looking at them."

He sighed, and looked at me like I was an innocent child. "Mary, there are times when the only way to get ahead in this world is to break a few bones. It's not something I prefer to do myself, so I use men who can do it for me."

But it was more than breaking bones. I came upon him one day when he was sitting with a sallow little man who was wearing an expensive suit. The man didn't smile when Aloysius introduced him to me. He simply nodded his head and looked me up and down like I was a piece of meat hanging in a butcher shop.

"This is Mr. Raphael," Aloysius said. "He is an associate of mine, who is helping me solve a problem."

I knew it was serious business, because they went back to their discussion and it was all done in hushed voices. I saw Aloysius hand over a wad of cash to the man, and the fellow smiled and showed a gold tooth in the front of his mouth. When he got up to leave, his jacket fell open and I saw the hilt of a nasty looking knife in a case on his belt. I had no illusions that he would not use it.

When he left I asked Aloysius what that man was going to do.

"Why, I told you, he's fixing a problem for me," Aloysius said.

"What do you mean, 'fixing'?" I said. "Tell me straight, O'Toole, is he killing someone for you?"

He looked at me with those cold eyes and said, "He's helping with a problem. It will be solved by tomorrow morning."

That was it for me. I'd seen lives ruined from the opium trade, but so far I didn't have murder on my conscience. Now I knew I was sleeping with a man who had no hesitation in ordering someone murdered if it pleased him.

It made me shudder inside, and it was then I decided to leave for good.

But where would I go? I had no one who would take me in. I wasn't associating with saints these days -- everyone around me was tainted in some way. I despaired of ever finding a way out of this life, but at the same time I knew I couldn't go on.

It was a Tuesday when Aloysius told me about the murder, and the next morning I got up early and took a trolley to St. Malachy's, a church I'd heard about from some of my friends among the serving girls. It was on 11th street near Girard Avenue, an old church frequented by the Irish laboring class, and far enough away from Center City that I wouldn't run into anyone who knew Aloysius.

When I went in there were only a few old women muttering their prayers in the pews, and I went straight down to the statue of Mary, her face full of hope and sadness at the same time, and I prayed to her.

"I'm not one for prayer, as you know," I whispered. "But I'm a mother too, so maybe I can talk to you as one mother to another. I

49

pray that my boy is safe in this wicked world, that he has people who love him, and that he doesn't hate me for what I've done. And I pray that you would help me to find a way out of this mess I'm in. Lord knows I've done bad things, and my soul is sick with grief and guilt. I need to get away before it kills me. I'm sorry for what I've done, but I beg you to get me away from Aloysius O'Toole before I do worse. I have no one to turn to. You're my only hope."

I finished my prayers and walked down the aisle with a heavy heart, not knowing if the Lady would answer me. I went through the wooden doors to the vestibule and walked straight into a priest who was coming through, and I knocked him down. I'm a substantial woman, as I've said before, and he was a man in his fifties, thin as a reed, and it was plain he didn't believe in such things as eating for pleasure.

"Sorry, Father," I said, pulling the old boy up. "I was thinking about my own problems, I reckon, and I wasn't paying attention."

"Why, that's no problem," he said, in a brogue as thick as County Down. "I'm not the worse for a bit of a fall."

"I recognize that accent," I said. "It's Tipperary you're from, sure as my name is Mary Driscoll."

"That it is," he said. "I was born in Clonmel, the prettiest town in all of Ireland."

"You'll get an argument from me about that," I said, "for I was born in Skibbereen, in Cork, and it's only a skip and a jump to the tip of Ireland, where we get the balmy sea breezes and the sunshine."

"Sunshine!" says he. "I think your memory is flawed, Mary Driscoll, or else the climate has changed dramatically since I moved away when I was a boy."

"Well, I admit sunshine is a bit scarce in our country," I said. "But you'll find a wee bit more of it down where I come from."

He smiled, and it was clear he was tickled by my humor. I looked him over, and I pegged him for one of these scholar types, with a long nose and a high forehead, and he certainly carried himself like a man who was used to standing in front of a classroom and lecturing. It was clear from his soft hands that he hadn't done much with them besides turning the pages of a book. Still, he had a kind look in his soft brown eyes, and I liked him.

He looked a bit lonesome, in the way that a scholar can be, I suppose, with nothing to keep him company but his books.

"What's the news from Skibbereen, then?" he said. "Is it long since you came over?"

"It's been twenty years, Father," I said. "And I haven't been back since. I hear the latest gossip from my friends over here. It's brilliant how fast the news travels, you know. But I haven't been to visit in many a year. I don't miss it, not with the troubles they're having now."

"Yes," he said, his brow furrowing and a pained look about his lips. "I think that England won't let our people be free without a bloody fight. I fear for the safety of our countrymen."

"Well, I haven't energy to get caught up in that," I said. "I've had enough trouble keeping body and soul together over here, to be honest. I'm hanging on by my fingertips, I am."

51

He looked me up and down, and smiled. "I wouldn't say you're doing badly, Mary Driscoll, from the way you're dressed. I don't know much about women's clothes, but that dress you're wearing looks like it comes from a fine shop. Why, I'd think you were one of these grand ladies in their carriages on Chestnut Street if I didn't know better."

I've always been one to appreciate a compliment, and I gave him a smile and a curtsey. "Thank you, Father," I said. "Priest though you are, you've learned how to flatter a woman, and that's no small skill." I shook my head and frowned, though. "But it's not my worldly goods I'm worried about. It's my soul."

At that his face clouded and he folded his hands together as if he were praying. "That's a serious thing to say, Mary, and me a priest. If you have a grave sin on your soul, let me hear your Confession. You shouldn't walk about with something like that on your conscience. The confessional is right inside the church. I'm late for an appointment with the archbishop, but it can wait. There's nothing more important than confessing a mortal sin."

"I haven't been to Confession in many a year," I said. "You'd better go to your appointment, Father. You don't have time to hear me out."

He leaned over and put his hand on my shoulder, and said, "My child, I have all the time in the world. Please, come in and unburden your soul."

Maybe it was the kindness in his voice, but I followed him into the church, and then into the dark wooden confessional, and when he slid the panel over and said the blessing and asked me to confess, it all came pouring out. I held nothing back, telling him of my stealing, my lies, the sins I committed with men, and all the bad

52

things I'd done since meeting Aloysius O'Toole. I thought my tongue would give out from all the exercise of telling my list of sins. Finally I was finished, and he spoke to me for a long time about how God would forgive me. I had to mend my ways, though, he said gravely.

"That's easier said than done, Father," I said, "I can't just go back and tell the man I'm working for that I don't care to be associated with him anymore. He's a dangerous man, and a vengeful one, and he'll come after me, sure. He's killed men, I know that, or at least he's given the order to kill them. He won't think twice about killing me, I know that as sure as I'm sitting across from you."

"Have you no place to go?" he said. "No one who could take you in?"

"Not a soul," I said.

"Why not go back to Ireland? That would be far enough away, wouldn't it?"

"I can't go back there, Father. I promised myself I'd never go back to the miserable life I had, and I just can't bring myself to crawl back there a failure."

He paused, seeming to think it over. "Can you cook?" he said.

"That I can," I said. "I was cook for a boarding house full of hungry men for a couple of years. I can make a meal fit for a hungry crew of men."

"I have a connection at the seminary," he said. "I have an office there, and affairs of the church have me out there several times a week. I know they've been looking for a good cook, to feed the seminarians. They had one quit a month ago, and they've been looking to replace her, since they need an extra hand in the kitchen. Could you cook for a group of seminarians and teachers? It would be no less than 60 men every night."

"If I could cook for those micks who worked on the docks and the streets, I can cook for a bunch of boys in priest school," I said.

"Good," he said. "You can stay in the rectory tonight, and I'll take you out to the seminary first thing tomorrow morning. They can give you a room and a small wage, and your meals will be free. Do you have any clothes you need to bring?"

"I've no wish to go back to my old haunts," I said. "If it's all right with you, I'll buy some clothes tomorrow with the money I have on me, and I'll not go back to Aloysius O'Toole. We can go to the seminary in the afternoon, when I have everything I need."

"Done," he said. "Now let me give the absolution, and you can join me for dinner."

And that was how the chapter of my life in the seminary began.

CHAPTER EIGHT

I never went back to the shop, and even though I hated to leave all the fine dresses there, I had no wish to see Aloysius anymore. I thought it would be the better policy to vanish from his life completely, and try to start fresh. Living at the seminary was as good as moving to China, as far as he was concerned. Aloysius would never have reason to visit a place where priests lived, I thought.

I was wrong, as it turned out, but more about that later.

This Bishop Prendergast (I quickly found out he was more posh than a common priest) was an important figure in the priestly world of Philadelphia, it seemed. Besides being the pastor of St. Malachy's, he had the important title of Auxiliary Bishop, and he was mixed up with all sorts of business for the head man downtown. He also came out to the seminary to teach and do various other jobs. I could tell he was important from the way the priests treated him, the reverence in their eyes when they spoke to him.

He was a quiet, reserved, thoughtful man, but I could tell he liked me because I made him laugh. Maybe I reminded him of the Ireland he left as a boy.

He sat next to me on the train out to the seminary, and he pointed to the green fields we were passing, and asked if they reminded me of the country back in Ireland.

"To be sure, and it's not a good memory," I said, sitting next to him as the train rattled on its way through the countryside. "I see lots of cows out there, and it reminds me that I told myself as a child I never wanted to see the backside of one of those creatures again. I used to have to get up at an ungodly hour to milk the few skinny cows my family owned. They gave a paltry amount of milk for all the work they required, and I thought it was nothing but a losing proposition to keep such animals. I wouldn't want to find myself in that position again."

He chuckled. "We don't have that much control over where we end up, Mary. We must do the best with what God offers us."

"True," I said, "but if He doesn't offer me much worth considering, I can always ask Him for something different, can't I? I expect He's open to a little negotiating."

This time he laughed. "Well, maybe so, Mary. A woman with the gift of gab like yourself just might be able to negotiate a better deal."

When we got to the seminary, I was impressed with the massive stone buildings, the well-kept grounds, and the beautiful chapel with its stained glass windows. Bishop Prendergast took me to the kitchen to speak to Hilda Stein, a big-armed German woman with steel gray hair in a tight bun, and a stern look in her eyes. He'd already told me she was "a bit hard to work for," as he put it, and that they'd had trouble keeping cooks because of her.

She took me to a small office near the kitchen, and it was hardly bigger than a closet. She had a desk and two chairs, and she told me to sit while she asked me questions. I wasn't interested in baring my soul to her about stealing Mrs. Lancaster's jewelry, so I made up a story that I had been a domestic servant for a few years, but then I tired of it and tried my hand at other occupations.

"Do you have references?" she said.

"None," I said.

She looked at me with an upraised eyebrow. "Why not?"

"I didn't see the need for them. I know my worth. I don't need any employer to offer opinions about my work habits or my honesty."

She looked at me like I was some strange new kind of vegetable a local farmer was trying to sell. "I've never hired someone without references."

"Well, there's always a first time," I said, folding my arms. I wasn't going to let her intimidate me.

She stared at me for a full minute, then she shook her head and clucked for a time, but finally seemed to come around. "It's a bit irregular, and I wouldn't do it for anyone else, but Bishop Prendergast himself has recommended you to me, and that man carries a lot of weight around here. People say he'll be the next Archbishop in the diocese, and he's very well liked. If he says you'll do well, I guess I can take a chance on you."

"It's a decision you won't regret," I said. "I'll do a fine job for these junior priests out here. I know how to keep them well fed."

"Ha!" she said. "You have a lot to learn about working in a seminary. For one thing, they're not priests yet. They're studying to be priests, but it takes years. Most of them are nowhere near graduation, and they're boys, not men, so you'll do better to remember that."

"That I will," I said. "It looks like I'll be undergoing my own course of study here."

And I did learn a lot about priests, and what it takes to become one, in my time at the seminary. I saw that they weren't so different from regular folks, and that was the biggest surprise. Back in Ireland, the people looked at a priest as if he was a living saint, one step below Jesus Himself. Living around these men, I saw they had the same fears and doubts and flaws as any regular Tom or Patrick who goes to work every day and wakes up in the middle of the night wondering what it all means.

Oh, they weren't keen to show that side of it, to be sure. There was precious little questioning or discussion in their studies, it seemed to me. They knew all the prayers, and all the answers to the theology questions, by heart. I used to see them with their heads in their books, some of them with their lips moving, as if they were trying to burn all the words into their brains.

But there were other times when I could see the questioning in their eyes.

When I finished my day's work I used to like to take a walk around the grounds if the weather was good, for the place had acres of ground, with wide lawns and wooded areas, and a garden in the back that sloped down to a little creek. I liked to go there and meditate, as the priests called it. I don't know what meditating meant to them, but to me it was a time to think about my life and some of the choices I'd made. I'd often look at the patterns of the light in the clouds made by the setting sun, and I'd wonder if my Luke was somewhere looking at those same patterns. I thought about him often, and prayed every night that I'd meet him some day, though I feared he'd hate me for abandoning him the way I did.

One night when I was sitting on the wooden bench by the pond where I liked to watch the sunset, I heard a noise and turned to see a fellow in a black robe staring at me. He looked barely old enough to shave, and he had blond hair that was cut short on the sides and hung down in front of his face near his eyebrows. He was blushing, probably because I'd caught him staring at me. I suppose I was an exotic creature to him, being a woman. Hilda Stein was the only other woman on the premises, and I fancied myself a lot more attractive than her. She had a Teutonic look to her that put you in mind of those creatures you hear about in fairy tales, a great stone-faced troll that lives in the mountains. I wasn't a broth of a girl anymore, but I knew how to fix myself up, and I saw the boys looking at me sometimes, struggling with their thoughts. And this fellow was no different.

"Well, if you're here to look at the sunset, sit yourself down, boy," I said. "This bench is the best spot on the whole property for seeing it."

He stammered a bit, like he was in the presence of royalty, or something. "I, uh, didn't mean to intrude, it's just that I, uh, happened to be walking nearby, and--"

"Oh, stop your blather," I said. "You're wasting a precious moment here. If you keep talking like that, the sun will be gone and we'll miss the whole show. Sit down, I say, or leave me in peace to look at it."

He shuffled over and sat down on the edge of the bench, as far away as he could get from me without falling off. He seemed deeply uncomfortable, which amused me to no end.

"Now, that's better, isn't it?" I said. "Just look at that show, will you? It's better than a fireworks display, to my mind. It's God's own light show, wouldn't you say?"

"Yes," he said. "It's very beautiful. We get sunsets like this at home. I used to climb up to the top of our barn and look at them."

He had a wistful look in his eyes, and I said, "Where are you from, lad?"

"I'm from around Gettysburg," he said. "My family has a farm there. My grandfather came over from Sweden and settled there before the Civil War. It's a nice, peaceful place."

"Sweden, eh?" I said. "I never heard of many Roman Catholics coming from Sweden."

"There aren't many," he said. "In fact, most of my family is Lutheran. My mother is Catholic, though. She's not Swedish, she's Irish. My parents met when my mother came to Philadelphia to work as a servant. My Dad met her at the farmer's market at the Reading Terminal, where his family had a produce stand. He used to come in once a week to work at the stand, and that's where they met. She was buying groceries for her employer."

"Well, I admire your mother, marrying out of her faith," I said. "Not many's the woman who's strong enough to do that."

His face clouded over, and for a moment I thought he was going to cry.

"She's gone now," he said. "She died ten years ago, of the consumption. I was thirteen. She just wasted away for years, and I could hardly stand it. It was terrible."

"I'm certain it was," I said. I leaned over and put my hand on his and gave it a squeeze. He seemed like he needed a woman's comforting touch just then, and he must have, for he squeezed my hand back hard.

"She wanted nothing more than that her son should be a priest," he said. "It seemed to be the only thing that would comfort her. So, I told her I'd made a decision to go in the seminary. I remember the smile on her face when I told her. It was only a week before she died. I think it helped her die in peace."

"I'll wager it did," I said. "But how do you feel about it? It's a big decision, my boy, and do you think it was the right one?"

"What I think doesn't matter," he said, spitting out the words. "I promised her, practically on her deathbed. I must do it for her, I must!"

The sun was almost below the horizon now, just a small red sliver of it was still visible, but its rays had turned the clouds just above it a riot of pink, orange, and red, and in the dying light I thought I saw a tear roll down his cheek. I patted his hand and said, "You're a good son, and I know you want to do right by your dear mother, but I don't think any of us should go through life trying to keep promises we made when we were barely more than children. Life has many twists and turns, and none of us know where it will take us. You're not the same person you are at 23 that you were at 13, and you shouldn't try to be."

He pulled his hand away and stood up. "I thank you for talking to me, madam, but I should be going back now. I have studying to do before bed. I wish you a good night."

"I didn't get your name," I said. "What do you call yourself?"

"Joseph," he said. "My name is Joseph Lindstrom."

"Very good, Joseph Lindstrom," I said. "I am glad to meet you. I come here most nights, so if you ever want to talk again, you are welcome to join me."

"Thank you," he said. "I may take you up on that offer."

I knew he would.

Joseph Lindstrom came back quite a few times and we had many a fine chat while looking at the sunset, or perhaps just watching the patterns of the clouds on an overcast evening. He valued my companionship, and I am sure he told me things he never revealed to anyone else, about his doubts and fears and the great sadness inside him. I tried to give him words of comfort and encouragement, as best I could, and I think it helped him. I told him it was not a good thing to live your life regretting a choice you'd made as a young and foolish person. I was thinking of how I gave away my little Luke, but I didn't tell him that.

I've spent a lot of time observing men in my life, and I learned a few things about them along the way. The biggest thing I learned is that they're all thick, mule-headed creatures, and if you leave them to themselves they usually make a mess of things. They need a woman to set them straight, and it's a pitiable thing when they don't have one around, or they won't listen when they do.

The seminary is a good example. All those men thrown together in that place, and it was so plain to me that they missed the woman's touch in their lives. They did their studying, they built their castles in the air with their theology, they talked about how they were going to go out and win souls for God, oh, they had grand plans and goals, to be sure -- but it was all sound and fury, like little boys bragging to each other. They were so full of their ideals and their fire for God, they didn't look at the pebbles in their shoes. Leave it to a woman to take the sensible view, I say.

I didn't say much around the priests, mind you. I didn't give a fig for most of what they said from the pulpit, but of course I went to church when I had to, and I mouthed the prayers like a good churchwoman. I was getting three square meals a day, a warm bed to sleep in, and I was safe from the prying eyes of Aloysius O'Toole. I was not about to risk all that and to get myself sacked for a few trifling disagreements about rules and regulations.

So the years slipped by, and in the blink of an eye, it seemed to me, I was 45 years old. It was 1907, and it was an old maid I'd become. I often thought of my Luke, and I'd imagine him in the different stages of his life. He would have been close to 15 at that point, almost the age I was when I left the shores of Ireland. It was hard to believe Luke was almost an adult; the time had gone so fast. I wondered what he looked like, what he sounded like, if he'd found his way in life, if he'd had his first kiss. Sometimes I'd cry myself to sleep with thoughts like these, but in the morning I'd always wake up and put a smile on my face, for there's no use in moping about when you have work to do.

The years went on, and I expected that nothing would change for me, but then one day in 1908 they suddenly did. The church in Philadelphia was expanding, and Archbishop Ryan, who was the head man, was on a building campaign. The man had doubled the number of schools in less than twenty years, and there were more than a hundred schools now for teaching Philadelphia's Catholic boys and girls. He was on a mission to expand the archdiocese's buildings, and I often saw Bishop Prendergast at his side when he visited the seminary. Prendergast was his right hand man and dealt

63

with many of the companies that were building these new schools, hospitals, and other places.

With all that building in the city, they decided the seminary needed some work done too, and they started a building project. There were workers everywhere on the campus, throwing up buildings left and right.

And that's how I met Francis Dillon.

CHAPTER NINE

He was a fine, good man, wasn't he?

Francis Dillon was the boss of a crew of bricklayers, and I would never have met him except that a couple of his men stole food from my kitchen. I was standing over a hot stove making steak for the noontime meal, when I heard a noise behind me and I saw a couple of sunburned micks grabbing a whole hock of ham from a cutting board and making off with it.

"Stop, you dirty thieves," I yelled, and went after them with a meat cleaver in my hand. They probably didn't think a woman would give chase, but they didn't count on Mary Driscoll. I followed them out the back door of the kitchen and chased them across the lawn waving the cleaver, bellowing loud enough to raise the dead. They tried to hide behind a shrine to the Blessed Mother, a stone altar at one end of the garden, but I found them, and I was waving the cleaver at them with intentions of using it.

"Come out, you thieving ruffians, or I'll cut you to pieces right here on the altar!" I said.

I would have done it, too, except just then a voice behind me said, "Begod, is it murder I'm witnessing on the grounds of the seminary?"

I turned to see a shortish man in work clothes with a sunburned face, bushy sand-colored eyebrows, and a shock of red hair that was mixed with gray. He was looking at me like he couldn't believe his eyes.

65

"You've not witnessed murder yet, boyo, but you'll see it in a moment if those two rascals don't give me the ham back that they stole from my kitchen," I said, waving the cleaver in the direction of the two men.

"Let me handle this," he said, putting his finger to his lips to quiet me.

"All right," he said. "I want the two of you to show yourselves. Come out from behind that altar, both of you! I've an idea of who it is, but I want to see with my own eyes. Out with you!"

The two thieves stood up from behind the altar, and the both of them looked like they were ready for a fight. They had their chins sticking out and their chests puffed, and the taller one of them put the greasy lump of ham on the altar as if he were being made to give up what was rightfully his. He glared at me like I was the Devil himself, and I'd just stolen his dinner.

"Bannion and Turner," the man next to me said. "I thought as much. The two of you have done nothing but cause trouble since I hired you."

"It was just a ham," the taller one said. "These priests won't miss it, Francis. They eat like kings out here; we've seen it ourselves. Better to give it to a couple of men who work for a living, instead of these layabouts. Why, they're nothing but a bunch of leeches in this place."

The man named Francis walked straight over to the tall one and socked him in the jaw, knocking him into the bushes behind the altar. He had to reach up to do it, since he was shorter than the other man by half a foot. He didn't seem afraid of either one of the

66

ruffians, and he stood there glaring at them, his fists clenched at his sides.

"The both of you are fired," he said. "Tell Simmons to give you your pay. I'm giving you fifteen minutes to get off the grounds, or I'll thrash you both so hard your own mothers won't recognize you. Now, get out of my sight!"

The two men got up and disappeared so fast you'd have thought they had the hounds of Hell after them.

Francis lifted the ham off the altar and turned to me.

"I am sorry for the behavior of my workers," he said. "I should not have hired those two ignorant micks in the first place, but I was doing a favor to a friend, who asked me to give his relatives their first job in this country. If that's the kind of morals they have back in the old country these days, God help them. Well, I'll carry this piece of meat back to the kitchen. You may have to wash it off a bit, but I think it's still fit to eat."

"You got here in the nick of time, and I thank you for that," I said, as we walked back to the kitchen. "Another minute and I'd have murder on my soul, to be sure. What is your name?"

"Francis Dillon is my name, and don't be thanking me," he said. "I am sorry for all the trouble those two caused you. I didn't like the look of them when I hired them, always muttering to themselves in Gaelic and leering at things in this country like two hungry cats in a fish store. I tried to keep an eye on them always, and that is why I came looking for them. I've seen men like that before, and I know they're nothing but trouble."

"Well, you handled them pretty well," I said. "You seem to know how to handle yourself in a fight."

"I did a little boxing in my day," he said. "Just amateur stuff. I'm nothing special, Ma'am."

"My name is not Ma'am," I said. "Call me Mary Driscoll, if you please. And I don't know as I'd agree with you about the nothing special part."

He blushed when I said that, turning his sunburned face a shade of scarlet that would have done a tomato proud. It was charming, to be sure, to see how bashful he was around women. By the time we got back to the kitchen door I had only one question left.

"So, who is Mrs. Dillon, if I might ask?" I said. "A handsome fellow like you must have a wife. The girls would snatch a man like you up in a minute, I'd think."

His face got redder, and he broke out in a great perspiration. I was standing above him on the steps to the kitchen, and he seemed as if he wanted to disappear into the nearest hole in the ground.

"I've no wife, Mary," he said. "I never had much to offer a woman. I don't have much to say, as a rule, and women like a man who talks. I realized years ago there wasn't much hope for me in that department, so I just kept my head down and worked. I started my little bricklaying company, and I have a dozen men working for me, and that keeps me busy enough. Now I'm too old for a wife, I suppose."

"Don't sell yourself short, Francis Dillon," I said. "This world has a way of throwing surprises at us, and my policy is never to make my mind up about anything, for just when you do, something comes along to change it." I winked at him, and he blushed again.

It's a funny thing. I had been content for almost ten years working at that seminary with no man in my life. I thought Aloysius O'Toole had settled that issue for good. He was the only man I'd ever loved, but he was as poisonous to me as a snake's bite. It took a long time to get over him, and I'd finally reached a sort of contentment with my life. I thought I'd live at that priest factory till I was old and gray, and I'd die with a pack of them in their black skirts standing around my bed and muttering their prayers to send me off to Heaven -- or Hell, as the case might be. It was all planned out, you might say.

And then, in one moment, it all changed. I saw that I was tired of this life, tired of the sameness of it, tired of sleeping alone in my bed, and tired of living like an observer in my own life. I wanted companionship, conversation, and a bit of closeness with a man, and I saw I could get that with Francis Dillon. He was a lonely man who needed a woman in his life, and I was a lonely woman who needed a man -- so we could fix it all easily.

Francis didn't know it, of course, but I did. Men never realize what's good for them, so women have to take over in that department.

Francis Dillon was indeed a bashful man around women, like so many Irishmen. There were only two I'd ever met who seemed comfortable around a woman, Peter Morley and Aloysius O'Toole. Morley had a cheating heart, though, but at least he had a heart. That was the one thing Aloysius lacked. He was comfortable around women, but not because he had any feeling for them, it seemed to me. It was because he never felt threatened by anyone, man or woman, since he knew he could always get the upper hand.

After being with a man like that, though, Francis Dillon was as refreshing as a drink from a cool stream. Sure, he was a bashful man and didn't know what to say to me most of the time, but I knew he was as honest as the day was long and as solid as a 100-year-old oak tree. He came to see me every day at one o'clock, when the midday meal was done, and I'd pack a picnic lunch and sit out under a magnificent maple tree that overlooked the fields and lawns of the back end of the seminary. Hilda Stein didn't like me taking my lunch outside with a man, but she'd long since learned to curb her tongue, for I could put her in her place with a few choice words (some of them I knew she'd never heard from the priests).

I prodded Francis to tell me of his life, and he told me how he'd come to Philadelphia as a boy of ten with his parents, but his father had quickly fallen into bad habits involving whiskey and gambling, and one day he'd just disappeared. Francis had gone to work in a clothing mill, and had various other jobs along the way, just to help his mother pay the bills. They'd never lived in anything but rooming houses, and often had to leave in the middle of the night when they couldn't pay the rent. "We used to walk down Broad Street sometimes and I'd see the grand houses with their porches and their big fronts," he said, "and I thought they looked like castles. I always liked looking at houses, for I'd never had a place to call my own."

His mother died when he was only 16, and Francis was on his own from that day. A kindly old Irishman took pity on him and got him a job as a laborer for a bricklaying company, and that was how he learned his trade.

"It's been a good life," he said. "I have a name for doing good work, and I've never had a problem finding employment. It was only five years ago I decided to start my own little company, and praise God, we've been able to stay busy. There's enough work to keep food on my table and a roof over my head, and that's fine with me."

"Why, there's more than that, man," I said. "This Archbishop Ryan is quite the builder, they say. They're breaking ground every week on new schools, churches, and hospitals. You could do a land office business just for him, I'd think."

He laughed and shook his head. "Oh, no, Mary. I don't set my sights that high. I'd have to hire more men, start a bigger operation, and it would be too much. I'm just a poor working fellow, not a man of business. I'm happy with my little slice of work."

"Well, that's shortsighted, if you ask me," I said. "What's the use in staying small when you could be big? Isn't that why your parents came over here, man? For an opportunity they couldn't get back in Ireland? A fellow who thinks like you do could have stayed back in Ireland on his little patch of ground, eating potatoes and trying to keep the pigs out of his little thatch-roofed shanty. Don't you want to live in one of those grand houses on Broad Street?"

"I'm not smart enough to run a big operation," he said.

"That's where I come in," I said. "I've got the brains to help you out, Francis. I know I'm a woman, but I'm a sight smarter than most men I've ever met. You let me help you out, and I promise you'll be living in grand style within two years."

He grinned and shook his head. "You're the most amazing woman I've ever met, Mary, and you certainly have big ideas. It's a tempting offer, but what would it look like to have a woman in charge of my operation? I don't think it would sit well with the archdiocese."

"Don't you worry about that," I said. "I've lived with these black skirts long enough, and I know how to handle them. And besides, we'll make it all nice and official. We'll become man and wife."

At that moment Francis looked like he was about to have a heart attack. His face reddened and his eyes bugged out, and his lips moved but no sound came out. I suppose it was upsetting for the poor man to have a woman propose marriage to him like that, but I wasn't going to shilly-shally around about it. I could see lots of advantages to us teaming up in that way, and I thought it was time to sign the papers and get on with it.

"But, Mary," he said, when he was finally able to speak. "Are you saying we should get. . . I mean, that we should. . . well, what I want to say is--"

"Yes, I just proposed to you, Francis Dillon," I said. "To make it plain: I'm saying we should get married. I know it's a bit irregular for a woman to bring up the subject like that, but I'm not of an age to dance around about such things. I think we should get the ball rolling, and that's that."

"I don't know," he said. "It isn't that I'm not fond of you, Mary. Lord knows it would be a comfort to see you every day. But it's just that I thought I was done with the idea of marriage. I thought I was past--"

"Well, get the idea back in your head, man," I said. "You're not too old to tie the knot, and neither am I. Unless of course, you don't want me."

I tossed my head, and then looked away, giving him a good look at my profile, making sure to show him my best side.

"No, Mary," he said, suddenly grasping my hand with his calloused mitts. "No, it's not that I don't want you, not at all. Why, I count it a blessing from God above that you'd want to spend even one day with the likes of me. If you'll have me, Mary Driscoll, I'll be the happiest man alive to be your husband."

That settled it. We were married in a month.

CHAPTER TEN

When I went to the priests and told them I was leaving, they all clucked and said they'd miss my cooking. Some of them looked askance at me, for it was a puzzle to them, a woman of my age suddenly getting married. I told them I'd found my vocation late in life, and it was to be a wife to a good man like Francis Dillon, to make his meals and keep house for him.

I had no such idea in my head, of course. Oh, I'd cook his meals and make sure he had a respectable house to live in, but I was going to be a partner in Francis Dillon's business, of that you may be sure. I could see the situation clearly -- here was a man who did excellent work (I asked Bishop Prendergast himself, and he told me Francis had a reputation as one of the best bricklayers in the city), and yet he was running a small operation with only twelve men, just plodding along like a horse with blinders on. Why, there was a building boom going on in the archdiocese of Philadelphia, and they were breaking ground on new schools almost once a month. A good bricklayer like Francis could have his hands full of work, if he played his cards right.

And I was the woman to help him get that work. I spoke to Prendergast the first opportunity I had, knocking on the door of his office my last day at the seminary.

I sat down across from his desk and let him speak first.

"So are you leaving us, Mary?" he said, his long face looking mournful. "Is this the end of your stay with us?"

"Yes, Bishop," I said. "'Tis a sad day, for I've enjoyed my time here, but all things must change, I suppose. I've met a good man in Francis Dillon, and we are going to be married. I've arranged for us to be married in the chapel at the cathedral, in two weeks on Tuesday. I'd be honored if you'd come."

He raised an eyebrow. "The cathedral, Mary? And how did you manage that? I thought that was reserved for the high and mighty in this city, to marry off their daughters and make a big show of it."

I laughed. "Yes, it's a bit of a rare atmosphere for Mary Driscoll from Skibbereen, I suppose, but I promise not to ruin any of the furniture. I won't have any low class shanty Irish mucking up the place. 'Tis a small wedding, with just a few close friends."

He broke into a grin. "Oh, I know you'll take good care of the place, Mary. I wouldn't expect you to have anyone spitting in the aisles. Is this Francis Dillon a good man? I know he's a good bricklayer, but will he make a good husband?"

"The finest," I said. "He's a bit long in the tooth, like myself, but he's not too old that I can't train him up right. He has good intentions, and that's what counts."

"Good," he said. "Then I'll be happy to come to your wedding, Mary."

"There's one other thing," I said. "You said yourself Francis is a good bricklayer. I know he does fine work, and he's well respected. The man should be further along in his enterprise than he is, though. He's got a small operation, but I just know he could handle something bigger. I was wondering if you could find some bigger jobs for him, maybe one of these schools you're building every week."

He cocked an eyebrow at me. "Why, Mary, are you already running his business? I thought it was a wife you were going to be, not his business manager."

"I'm just trying to help the man I'm marrying put food on the table," I said. "There's nothing wrong with that, is there? Why, people have to look out for themselves in this world."

He folded his hands in front of his chest and examined me through his steel-rimmed glasses. "No, I suppose there's nothing wrong with trying to help your husband put food on the table. But the kind of bricklayers I deal with for a big project like a school have a lot more than twelve men working for them, Mary. A little operation like the one Francis runs couldn't handle the work."

"You let me handle that, Bishop," I said. "I know he needs to hire more men, but we'll find them, don't worry yourself about that. I'll sort things out for Francis."

"Oh, I'm sure you will, Mary," he said, grinning again. "One thing I know about you is you can get things done. My only question is, does Francis know about this plan? Did you let him in on your big idea for his business?"

I chuckled. "Well, he's not entirely up on all the details, Bishop, I'll admit. I wanted to speak with you first, before I broke the news to him. But don't worry, he'll be fine with the plan once I have a talk with him."

"Ah, Mary," he said, shaking his head and grinning once more. "It's always a treat to speak with you. You get right to the heart of the matter, and it's a breath of fresh air for a man like me, who deals with so many people who use their words to confuse the issue. I will miss my talks with you. All right, I'll see what I can do about putting Francis on the list of contractors for one of the projects coming up. I'll take your word for it that he'll be able to handle the job, and his work will be satisfactory."

"It'll be more than satisfactory, Bishop," I said. "It will be excellent, and you'll want to use him for all your jobs, I guarantee. Now, if you'll give me your blessing, I'll go tell Francis his life is going to change."

He looked at me ruefully and said, "The poor man, maybe I should be giving him a blessing, for he'll need God's help, I expect. Be that as it may, bow your head, Mary, and I'll give you my blessing."

I bowed my head and he said a blessing over me. I was glad to have it, for it's always good to get a blessing when you start a new page in your life. You can't forget to use your brains, of course, but a blessing helps.

The wedding was a small affair, but I was happy nonetheless. Francis looked uncomfortable in his new suit of clothes, with his hair plastered to his head and his collar tight around his sunburned neck. The look in his eyes when he promised to take me as his wife was pure joy, though, and it touched me. The man was so in love with me, and that pleased me very much. I reckoned that no one, man or woman, had loved me like that, not even my mother when she held me in her arms back in Ireland.

I'm ashamed to say I didn't love him like that, however. Then again, there was no one I loved like that, save my boy Luke. Next to my love for him, everything else was just a thimbleful of water compared to the ocean itself. I knew Francis was a good, decent man, and I respected him greatly for it. There are few enough of those kind of men in the world, and I wanted to do right by him. I was determined to make a good life for us both, and I knew I'd make him happy.

But love? No. The only other person I'd felt love for -- and it was more lust than love, I suppose -- was Aloysius O'Toole. But it had been ten years since I'd seen that devilish handsome face of his, and I knew it was better for me, body and soul, to be out of his presence. There is a kind of love that will kill you, sure as if you were suffering little cuts every day, slowly bleeding to death, and that's what loving Aloysius was for me.

No, Francis was the better man by far. I didn't have a physical attraction to him, but we had a sort of understanding about that. For our honeymoon we went to Atlantic City for three days, staying in a grand hotel on the boardwalk, and on the first night Francis came to me in bed naked as the day he was born.

"And what is this?" I said, feeling his rough skin rubbing up against me.

"Well, Mary," he said. "I thought since it was our wedding night, this is what I'm expected to do. If it's your pleasure, I mean. I've no wish to offend you."

I turned and lit the lamp next to our bed, sending shadows flickering on the birds and flowers of the fancy wallpaper, then I put my hands on his face and looked into those innocent eyes of his.

"Francis, I love you as much as I can love a man," I said. "But I'm not a young woman anymore, and I have no wish to engage in the foolishness of a young woman. Those lamps have gone out inside me, and I don't think they can ever be lit again. I'll love you like no other woman has ever done, but I can't make my body do something it has no wish to do. Do you understand me, Francis?"

78

His face fell and there was hurt in his eyes, but he quickly mastered himself. "I understand you perfectly, Mary," he said, finally. "And I have no wish to force myself upon you. You're the queen of my heart, Mary, and I'll do whatever you wish. 'Tis enough for me to be near you like this -- it gladdens my heart like nothing I've ever felt before."

And there you have it. We came to an understanding, if you want to call it that. We would live together as man and wife, and we had an affection for each that was deep and wide, but we would never express it with our bodies. Instead, we expressed it in a thousand other ways. We had an easy and comfortable way with each other, and we were always touching, even kissing at times, falling asleep with our arms around each other every night. There was just nothing further, for we both knew there was no point in going down that road.

You may say it was an odd way for a husband and wife to behave, but I can read the signs of people's bodies very well, and it's clear to me that there are many long-married couples who act like strangers to each other. Why, you have only too look at them to see they barely touch each other, and the men prefer the company of other men, and the women of women. All those working men who spend their free hours in a saloon, and the women gossiping among themselves on their front porches or backyards -- they have more real affection for their companions than they do for their wives or husbands. I've heard enough of the gossip of women, and I knew the secrets of men from my wild youth, and I knew there was precious little going on between the bodies of quite a few married people.

No, Francis and I had it better than that. We enjoyed each other's company. We bought a little row house in Southwest Philadelphia, and it was our castle. Francis would come home at night and tell me everything that happened on the jobs, and I'd advise him on what I thought he should do to run his business better. As time went on I got more and more involved. I taught myself bookkeeping, so I could make sure he was accounting for all the money that came in and went out, and I did the talking when it came to dealing with the people in the archdiocese: the architects, the builders, the priests and the nuns who were running the schools. In time I even helped him with the hiring of his men, and he always said I had a sixth sense for finding honest fellows. I didn't tell him I had learned that lesson working in the Tenderloin. I could spot a lying man from 90 yards away, and I was never wrong.

In time my brains and Francis's reputation for good work brought us more and more business, and we had to keep expanding. Soon we had 50 men working for us, and we kept hiring more. I talked Francis into buying a commercial building by the river, where we could have shipments of bricks sent to us, and we could inspect them to make sure they were high quality. I even convinced him to buy motor trucks instead of the horse drawn wagons he was using, and I had them painted in bright green, with red letters that said, "Build Your Dreams With Dillon's Brickwork".

In 1913 Bishop Prendergast was made Archbishop of Philadelphia, and now I was friends with the most powerful priest in the city. We were going from one success to another, and things seemed like they were only going to keep going upward.

And that's when the trouble started.

CHAPTER ELEVEN

For a while it seemed as if nothing could go wrong. We went from success to success, and before long we moved out of our row house and into a bigger single home in a better neighborhood. I was wearing better clothes, and we bought a new Duesenberg, an extravagant motor car to be sure, but I told Francis it made us look successful, and it helped the business if we looked like we had the sheen of success on us. I got him to stop dressing in overalls and grimy work shirts, and I made him wear fine suits when we went to meet with the building committees and the bigwigs in the archdiocese.

In 1918 Archbishop Prendergast died, and I mourned the loss of this gentle man. It did no damage to Dillon's Brickwork, though, because he was replaced by Dennis Dougherty, a stocky Irishman from the coal fields of Scranton, and I knew him well. "Dinny", as he was affectionately called, was a teacher at the seminary when I worked there, and I'd made his acquaintance. He was a no-nonsense man who was much more the man of action than Prendergast, and when Francis and I called on him a few weeks after his installation, it was obvious he was planning big things.

He was sitting behind a great oak desk, his black cassock tight across the muscles of his shoulders, and he had a look like a caged animal. He seemed like he was itching to get outside, away from the confines of the office. He was drumming his fingers on the desk, impatient to get the conversation over with.

He looked at Francis, not me, and he said: "This archdiocese is growing like wildfire. The last two archbishops tried to keep pace with all the immigrants pouring into the city, but it wasn't enough.

The city is exploding with Catholics. I have parishes opening all over the place, and they don't have enough buildings to serve their people. We need schools, churches, offices, meeting halls, and the like. I am going to do everything in my power to meet the needs of my flock, and I'm going to expand the building program. Can you help me with this, Dillon?"

"Yes we can," I answered. "You just tell us what you need, and we'll provide it."

Dougherty looked at me in amazement, like I was a talking monkey or some such outrageous creature, and then he looked back at Francis, as if to ask, "What's going on here?"

Francis just shrugged his shoulders, and said, "Mary handles a lot of our management, Archbishop."

"Do you?" the archbishop said, raising his eyebrows and casting a glance my way. "I didn't think women got involved in running a man's business."

"She's smart as a whip, Archbishop," Francis said. "I wouldn't be where I am today without her."

Dougherty frowned and studied me more closely, trying to make up his mind. Then, he seemed to decide, and he sat back in his chair. "Well, it's irregular, but I'm not going to tell you how to run your business. What about it, though? I know you've done a lot of work for us, but what I'm planning will be a step up. You'll need a bigger operation, or you won't be able to keep pace."

"We'll find the men and train them," I said. "Don't you worry about that. We've done it before, and we can do it again. We'll be able to handle as much work as you can throw at us. And you know that Francis Dillon does fine work, Dinny. Not a complaint will you have when he's finished with his brickwork."

I used his nickname, Dinny, just to let him know I remembered him from the seminary, before he got so high and mighty. His face registered shock, but then his eyes flickered and I could see he remembered me.

"Why, Mary," he said, smiling. "I am sorry I didn't recognize you at first. You used to cook at the seminary, am I right? You've come a long way from then, haven't you?"

"I suppose we all have," I said, winking at him. "But it just goes to show that we all have more in us than we show in our younger years. God has given us many talents, hasn't He?"

"That He has, Mary," he said. He slapped the desk once and stood up, signaling the meeting was over. "I'll have the man in charge of the building program meet with you, and he'll go over the plans for the next couple of years. There are big things coming, Mary. It's going to be an exciting time."

I left that meeting feeling light as a feather, and I never knew such happiness. For the first time I finally started to feel secure, as if I had made it to the top of the mountain. I was finally rid of my past, after all these years.

And then I found out I needed the past to save me.

It happened fast, and without warning. One evening Francis told me he'd been visited on a job by some well-dressed men who wanted a word with him. They were Italian, he said, and spoke with accents. "They wanted me to hire some friends of theirs," he said. "I wasn't going to do that. You know yourself, Mary, my crews are all micks. They don't like Italians, and I can't afford to have problems on the jobs. Why, the men have to work as a team -- it all falls apart if they can't get along. I told them I had no need to hire any more men."

"What did these visitors say to that?" I asked.

"They told me I'd be sorry," Francis said. "I told them to get out of my sight or I'd beat them to a pulp. I wasn't going to let scum like that scare me."

Francis was not a man who scared easily, and I always admired that about him. Even so, I had a bad feeling about it. In my experience, you should pay attention to well-dressed men who threaten you. I had trouble sleeping for a few nights, but when nothing happened in a week, I relaxed a bit.

And that's when it happened. One afternoon I was sitting in the living room of my house, with ledger books spread out on the table in front of me, when there was a knock at the door. I went to answer it and saw Dooley McCourt, one of Francis' crew bosses, and he looked like he'd been through a whirlwind. His hair was a mess, he had blood on his torn clothing, and he had a wild look in his eyes.

"Mary, I've come to tell you that Francis has been hurt," he said. "He's been stabbed, and they took him to the Pennsylvania Hospital. Some gangsters showed up on the job in West Philadelphia, St. Anselm's School, and they pulled knives on Francis and carved him up. We caught one of them and beat him pretty bad, but the other one got away. I've got the truck outside -- you'd better come with me to the hospital."

I'm not a woman who cries, but when I walked into that hospital room and saw Francis bandaged like an Egyptian mummy, it took all my strength not to let the tears come streaming down my face.

A nurse in a white uniform came over and held my arm. "He's lost a lot of blood," she said. "He'll have a bad night tonight, but the doctors think he'll make it."

I bent down and put my hand in his palm, and Francis squeezed it, as if to say he'd be all right. I wanted to throw my arms around him, but I dare not. The nurse ushered me out of the room, telling me he needed his rest. I sat in a chair outside his room and let the tears come, my head in my hands and my body shaking like I had a deathly fever.

Dooley McCourt stood there, not knowing what to do. "I'm sorry it happened, Mrs. Driscoll," he said. "I saw them fellows come over to Mr. Driscoll, and they had words with him. He started to walk away, but quick as you please, the scoundrels were on him, and by the time I got there he was in pretty bad shape. If I was you, I'd tell the police about it. Maybe they'll catch the villains."

I knew better. We had come up in the world, to be sure, but to the police we were still ignorant Irish, not worthy of justice. The cops on the beat were Irish, and they'd be on our side, but there would be no use expecting the higher ups to care about a brawl on a building lot, even if there were knives involved. I knew we'd have no justice from them.

No, I'd have to take matters into my own hands if I wanted to avenge what happened. I knew there was only one path open to me.

Aloysius O'Toole.

CHAPTER TWELVE

He was waiting for you, wasn't he?

I figured Aloysius was still around -- he was too smart to get thrown in jail, and too tough to be killed. I hadn't seen him in fifteen years, but I knew it wouldn't take me long to find him.

I asked McCourt if he gambled.

"Why, no, Mrs. Driscoll, I wouldn't do a thing like that," he said, shuffling his feet and looking abashed. "It's a sin, isn't it? I wouldn't want that stain on my immortal soul."

"Don't be lying to me, Dooley," I said. "I know that men like to bet on horses and cockfights, and they find God knows how many other ways to lose their money. I know there are places in this city where you can do all of that. I want you to take me where you go to place a bet."

He was horrified. "Oh, Mrs. Driscoll, I couldn't do a thing like that! A woman like you, in a place like that -- no, it wouldn't be right. I could never--"

"Then you'll do something else for me, man," I said. "And if you tell me no this time I'll have Francis fire you for drinking on the job. Don't think I can't smell the whiskey on you, even if you've been sucking on lemon drops the last hour to hide it. I've got a nose for whiskey, and I know you've been tippling. I want you to take me to wherever Aloysius O'Toole camps out these days, and I want it done now. It's almost five o'clock, and that's quitting time. You take me there now."

"But Mrs. Driscoll," he said. "I don't know where he lives. I see him sometimes in places where I, ah, sometimes go of an evening. I'm just a poor working man, you see, and I don't frequent those places very much. He's not the type of man I call a friend, more of just an acquaintance, you'd say."

"I don't care what you call him," I said. "But as sure as I'm sitting here I know you've done business with him, in one way or another. He preys on people like you. Take me to him now, and make it quick."

And so Aloysius Declan O'Toole came back into my life, rising from the grave, you might say.

Dooley McCourt took me to a building in Chinatown. It was a brick building, and in the front there was a laundry. By the time we got there it was after 7:00 at night, and the place was closed. Dooley knocked on the door and an old Chinese man unlocked it and let us in, after scanning Dooley's face to make sure he recognized him.

The Chinese man looked askance at me, but Dooley reassured him with a nod of his head. "She's all right," he said. "We're here to see Mr. O'Toole."

The old man led us through a vast room with piles of clothing and washing tubs where other Chinese men paused in their work to look at me as if I was some new kind of animal, and when we got to the back he opened a door and led us up two flights of narrow metal steps, then knocked on a door. Another Chinese man opened the door, and the first one said something to him in their language, then he swung the door wide and let us in.

It was mostly dark in the room, except for the light from a bulb high in the ceiling, and at first I couldn't make out anything. Then, as we moved toward the light, I saw a man sitting at a table eating a meal. He had silver hair and he was a bit thicker than before, but I knew instantly it was Aloysius. My heart leaped in my chest, even though I tried to stay calm. Seeing him again called up all the old emotions.

He smiled when we came into his presence, and put his knife and fork down. I saw there was a bottle of red wine on the table, and two glasses in front of him.

"Well, well," he said. "If it's not my old friend Mary, come to visit me. Sit down, Mary, sit down. Your friend can wait downstairs." McCourt made some bowing and scraping motion and disappeared as fast as he could.

"Would you like a glass of wine?" Aloysius said. "It's a fine vintage, one of the best. Fresh off the boat from France. The war wreaked havoc on the French vineyards, but I have some friends who were able to tip me off that there were a few cases of good Burgundy coming in last week. And of course," he said, wiping his mouth with a white napkin, "I helped myself to them."

I sat down across from him at the table, but I waved the wine away. "None of your stolen wine for me," I said.

He frowned. "Now, Mary, let's not put too fine a point on it. I don't like the word 'stolen'. I prefer 'borrowed'. I'm just borrowing it, you see. Or, perhaps we could say I'm testing it, to make sure the French winemakers are back in top form again." He laughed and took another drink from the glass.

"You're a master at coming up with explanations, aren't you?" I said. "It's a nice way to describe what you do, Aloysius. You borrow lots of things. You just forget to return them."

He smiled, and a gold tooth in the front of his mouth flashed. He saw me looking at it, and said, "You've noticed my gold tooth, I see. It's a bit garish, I admit. I'm not a man who favors such things, as a rule, but it helps in my line of work. It impresses the common man, gives him the idea I'm a man of wealth and power. It's like a judge with his robes. He's just an ordinary man underneath them, but they give people the feeling that he has supernatural intelligence and gravity. Sometimes you have to play the game, Mary."

"Is that what you call it, Aloysius?" I said. "A game? If it's a game, it's one with bitter consequences for those who play it. I for one don't want to play that game."

He stared at me with those cold eyes, and I felt a shiver run through my body.

"When you left, Mary, it hurt my feelings," he said, suddenly playing the victim. "I thought I had been the soul of honesty and good intentions with you. I treated you very well didn't I? I like to think so. We had a good system going, but then all of a sudden you weren't there."

He leaned back in his chair and grinned at me. "Did you think you could just leave me like that, Mary? After all that had passed between us? Why, there was a time when I thought of walking right through the gates of that seminary and visiting you, girl, just to look you in the eye and hear you explain why you left."

Once again the chill ran through me. For so many years I thought I had escaped him, but now it was plain he knew where I was all the time.

He pushed his plate away, then pulled out a pack of cigarettes. He shook a cigarette out, then put it to his lips and struck a match from a box on the table. He lit the cigarette and blew a cloud of smoke in my direction. "I see it's dawning on you that I knew where you'd gone when you left," he said, slowly. "It's my business to know a lot of things in this city, and I have people who keep me informed. You see the extra wine glass on the table, Mary? I knew you'd be paying me a visit tonight. It's important for me to know things like that, as I said. Are you sure you won't have a glass of wine? It's quite good."

He held the glass toward me, but I pushed it away. "I'll not have it," I said, trying not to let the fear enter my voice.

"Fine," he said. He took a sip from his own glass, and then said, "So, what is on your mind, Mary?"

"I'm sure you already know," I answered. "My husband has been threatened by some ruffians, and I need to find a solution for this problem."

"Yes, I'm sorry about Francis Dillon's injuries," he said. "I hear he's a fine, upstanding man. It seems he runs quite a business, helping the priests to build schools all over this city. You've done well, Mary. But now, I hear you've got some nasty people who want to get involved in the running of this excellent operation you have. What a terrible world we live in!" He smiled sardonically.

"I came here because I thought you could help me," I said.

90

He took another sip of his wine, then looked at the ceiling, then straight at me. "Yes, I have an idea of how I can help you solve your problem, Mary. I could arrange things so that Francis never has to worry about a visit from those fellows again. You could sleep easy at night.

"There's just one thing, darling," he continued. "It will cost you."

I shrugged my shoulders. "Do you think I don't know that? There is a price on everything in your world, isn't there, Aloysius? Tell me, what is the price this time?"

"Well, Mary," he said, sitting back and folding his hands over his chest. "You know I'm a man of vision, and that's why I'm still in business. I think in grander terms than most of the fools who get into my line of work. I have no interest in the quick payday, like the rest of that lot, living from one job to the next, and barely staying out of jail. No, I've always used my brains to figure out bigger schemes. And I see something coming that will make everything I've done up to this point look as worthless as a tinker's damn."

He poured himself another glass of wine, then held the glass up to the light. "It involves this elixir, Mary. The drink of the gods, as the Greeks used to say." He took a sip, and smiled as he swallowed it.

"I'm sure you've heard the government has passed a law outlawing alcohol, Mary?" he said.

"That I have," I said. "I think Prohibition is a stupid idea, but it doesn't affect me so much. I'm not much of a woman for drink, as you know."

"You're right, the whole idea is mad," he said. "However, the fellows in Washington seem determined to try this experiment, which I am sure will be a total failure. You can't take a man's whiskey from him, Mary. He won't stand for it, and he'll find other ways to get it. And that," he said, with a smile on his face, "is where I come in. Why, this law is the best thing that ever happened to lads like me. I've got it all figured out, and I'll be the Whiskey King of this area before two years are gone."

"You're going to make illegal whiskey?" I said.

"Oh, no, not make it," he said. "That would be too easy a target for the police. I'd need equipment, supplies, and the men to make it work. No, there's too much chance for something to go wrong in that arrangement. I have an easier, safer plan than that. All I need to do is be the middleman between suppliers up in Canada, and the customers here in Philadelphia. I have some fast boats in my possession, faster than anything the authorities have, and all I have to do is arrange for my boats to pick up cargoes from ships out at sea, and slip into port in the wee hours of the morning, unload them and take them to buildings I own on the waterfront. Then, it's just a matter of getting my merchandise to the customers."

"You've got it all figured out, I see," I said.

"Oh, I think of all the details," he said. "I've got some of the men in blue on my payroll already, just to make sure there's no trouble when we start the operation next January, after this Prohibition law goes into effect."

"And what does this have to do with me?" I asked.

He smiled. "Mary, you're going to be my best salesperson! You've got all the best contacts, my girl. You're in tight with the high and mighty people in the archdiocese. All those years at the seminary did you good -- you can rub elbows with the people at the top of the ladder, can't you?"

"You mean the priests?" I said, incredulous. "Now, why would you think they'd be the people to sell your illegal whiskey to?"

He tapped a finger against his head. "Because I'm a man who thinks deeply, Mary. I know the archbishop and his cronies socialize with all the well to do Irish in this city. Yes, times have changed since you came over on the boat, haven't they? Back then the Irish were only fit to be serving girls and laborers, but it's different now. Some of those poor micks actually made something of themselves, and now they own businesses, they're politicians and doctors and lawyers. They live in big houses and they have their own servants. They're the ones paying for all these new schools and churches, aren't they? All the archbishop has to do when he wants to open a new St. Malachy's or St. Brendan's or Our Lady of Whatever is call up his friends in the top rung of the Knights of Columbus, and touch them for a few more thousand dollars. The archbishop and his entire inner circle go to parties at these people's houses all the time. And at parties you need whiskey, don't you?" He chuckled to himself. "No matter how high these Irishmen rise, they still want their whiskey, Mary."

"Are you seriously suggesting that I talk to the archbishop and ask him if I can sell him illegal whiskey?" I said. "Aloysius, I thought you were smarter than that."

He chuckled again, but there was no mirth in it. "No, I'm not suggesting that. The archbishop isn't going to buy his own whiskey, I know that. He has underlings who'll do it for him. No, I'm a man of subtlety, Mary. I always look for the less obvious way of doing things. What I want is for you, Mary Driscoll, and that husband Francis of yours to become part of the archbishop's circle, part of the ring of powerful people around him. Why, it's a step up in the world for you, Mary! You should be doing it already, even without me suggesting it to you. I hear you've got quite a successful bricklaying business, and you and Francis are raking in the money. It's time you acted the part, and began to socialize with the high and mighty in this town. That way you'll be in a position to get them whiskey when they need it."

"I can't just waltz into the archbishop's office and ask to be part of his social set," I said. "He doesn't invite the likes of me to his dinner parties. Francis and I do business with him, we're not his friends."

"Ah, but we can all use more friends, can't we?" he said. "The archbishop doesn't know you on a social basis, Mary, but I have no doubt he'll be happy to have you come to his parties. And I've taken care of that part, anyway. I have contacts downtown in his office. I know how to get you included on his social calendar, and I've already arranged it. There's a party at his residence in three weeks, and you're on the guest list. I presume that Francis will be recovered from his wounds by then. All you have to do, Mary, is put on a fine dress and get Francis into a respectable suit, and just be your charming self. Why, before you know it, you'll be an honored guest in all the best Irish homes in Philadelphia! All you have to do is enjoy yourself, Mary. I'll take care of the rest."

I shook my head. "You think of everything, don't you?" I said.

He smiled again, showing the gold tooth. "That I do, Mary. That I do."

"And you'll take care of this problem with the Italians?"

"It's as good as done. Those boys will never cross paths with Francis Dillon again, I promise you that." He held his hands wide and smiled. "See, it's simple, isn't it? All you do is go to parties with your husband, and I take care of your labor problems."

"Until when?" I said.

"Until I need you," he said, suddenly turning serious. "And then you do what I want."

And that was how Aloysius O'Toole came back into my life.

CHAPTER THIRTEEN

1919

I had to credit Aloysius; he took care of every detail. I was indeed on the guest list for Archbishop Dougherty's next party, and before long Francis and I were getting invited to many parties that involved powerful clergy and their rich Irish friends. We met builders and lawyers, manufacturers and tradesmen who'd made good. They were proud as peacocks of their success, and dressed in an imitation of the wealthy Protestants who'd kept them down for so long. These were people whose families had lived for generations on a patch of land in Ireland and lived on potatoes and a mouthful of milk from the family cow. They had grandparents who'd died in the Great Famine of the 1840s, and the memory of hunger was bred into them. They'd fought their way out of that miserable barefoot life, and they weren't ever going back. It was like a private club for people who had made it to the top of the mountain, and one you didn't get into unless you shared their story, their religion, their success.

And now Francis and I were in it.

I didn't hear anything from Aloysius for many months, but Francis had no more visits from the Italians, and things were going smoothly for the Dillon's Brickwork. Then, in December of 1919, Dooley McCourt showed up at my door with a note from Aloysius.

"Meet me tomorrow afternoon, when Francis is at work," it said. "Dooley will bring you to me."

I met him at his office in the warehouse district, and he went over the plan. In January, when Prohibition became the law of the land, all the bars and saloons would officially shut their doors, and all sales of alcohol except for medicinal purposes would stop.

"I want you to put the word out to your friends that you're able to supply them with whatever they need," Aloysius said. "Make it discreet, of course. We don't want to attract any attention to ourselves. Just let them know, Mary, that's all. Then, we'll sit back and wait."

I did as he told me, putting a word in the ear of the rich folks I knew, and before long I had a flow of orders for Aloysius. The women would take me aside in their grand houses, maybe to a little breakfast nook, or on their back porch, or even upstairs to their bedrooms, and they'd tell me what their husbands wanted for their next party. I've always had a good memory, and I just committed it all to my brain, rather than risk writing anything down. Then I'd get the word to Dooley McCourt, who'd stop by in his truck every Monday morning after Francis left for work. Dooley would write down all the orders, and he'd take them to Aloysius. In a few days he'd start off on his delivery route, and by the weekend all the fine people would have their liquor for their parties.

By the end of 1920 we were doing well, and by 1921 even better.

It was quite the life for Francis and I at those parties. Neither of us drank much liquor, but we saw lots of people getting out of their heads and doing wild things like climbing trees in their tuxedoes and evening gowns. It was a time of mad excess, the 1920s, and we saw a lot of it at the houses of the fine people.

But then one day things changed. I was sitting at the long dining table of Edward McGinty, a man who'd come from County Mayo as a boy and made money selling guns to the Army. He was in his 60s now, a stout, red-faced man with a bulbous nose that showed he enjoyed his whiskey. He had a waiter fill our glasses with an amber liquid, and he proposed a toast: "To good old Irish poteen," he said. "It has the taste of the old country in it."

I took a sip, and it was truly a remarkable thing. It was not your ordinary home brewed whiskey. This stuff had hints of flavor I'd never tasted in a whiskey before. It went down easy and gave you a warm glow all over.

"What is it?" I said, for I didn't recognize it as anything Aloysius sold.

"Oh, I was tipped off to this by a friend," McGinty said, smiling like he had a great secret that gave him an edge over us. "It's made right here in Philadelphia, by a man who learned the recipe back in Ireland. He's a treasure, that one. Isn't it amazing? I think he learned his trade from the fairies."

"To be sure, it's excellent stuff," I said.

"I think you have some competition, Mary," said Morris Wells, a financier sitting across from me. "This stuff would make you forget there was any other drink in the world."

I didn't tell Aloysius about it, figuring that McGinty knew he had a good thing going and wouldn't want to share his secret. But when I went to three other parties in the next month and found the same poteen served, I got the word to Aloysius that I wanted to meet with him.

"You've got competition," I said, without preliminaries, when I saw him. He was eating his lunch of fried oysters and clams, and he had a white cloth tied around his neck. He kept chewing for a full minute before answering me.

Then he put his knife and fork down, took a sip of his wine, and said, "Thank you for your concern, Mary, but I could have saved you a trip down here. I already know about the man who's making poteen. There's not much that happens in this city I don't know about, darling."

"He's running a small operation, from what I understand," I said.

"Yes it is small," he said, wiping his mouth with the napkin. "But I don't like competition, no matter how small. It's not the way to succeed in business. Why, John D. Rockefeller didn't build his fortune by welcoming competition, did he? No, he crushed his competition. I'm going to deal with this fellow, one way or another."

"Are you going to send your goons around to destroy his equipment?" I said. "Maybe break his legs? That would be like you, Aloysius."

"Why, Mary," he said, furrowing his brow. "I'm surprised at you, thinking such thoughts about me. I'm not a man of violence. There are times when it's necessary, of course, but I find there are other ways to persuade a man to do what I want. No, I want to hire the fellow, not break his legs. I've tasted his product, and it's excellent, fine stuff, the very best. I'm going to have him work for me."

"Maybe he won't want to work for you," I said.

He smiled. "Oh, I think he will. Actually, he's a man I think you know, Mary. His name -- well, the one he goes by now -- is James Francis. I think you know him as Peter Morley, though."

CHAPTER FOURTEEN

I felt like I'd been stabbed in the heart when Aloysius said that name. Peter Morley, the father of my Luke. It was a name I hadn't thought of for many a year, but I could never have forgotten it. I was still praying for Luke every night, praying for his health and safety, but I never mentioned the name "Peter Morley" in my prayers.

"So, that scoundrel is still alive, is he?" I said. "I'd have thought he died a long time ago, as payment for his cheating ways. I expected some wronged husband would have beaten him to death by now."

Aloysius flinched, just a bit, at my anger. "Why, Mary, I think you still have feelings for the man."

"My only feeling is hate," I spat. "He's the father of my only child, and I was forced to give my boy away twenty years ago. I made a mistake ever letting that man into my bed, and I've been paying for it ever since. I have no love for him. He was the husband, if you could use that word for a man like that, of Rose Sullivan, a girl I came over on the boat with. He did her wrong too, getting her with child before they were married. It serves her right, though, for she's the one who got me sacked for stealing, and set me off on the path I've taken. It's a measure of justice to me that Rose married that sewer rat. I'm sure she's had a rough time of it being married to him."

"You are correct," Aloysius said. "It hasn't been easy for poor Rose, but he left her long ago with the three sons he gave to her. He changed his name and married an English lass named Edith, and he's got another child. He's struggled in that marriage too. It seems your Peter can't stay put with one woman."

So he'd left Rose. I wasn't surprised, although I'd had a picture in my head of them married to this day. Well, then, Rose had suffered more than I thought. For as bad as it would be to be married to a cheating man like Peter Morley, it would have been much worse to have him leave her with three children. It wasn't easy for a woman with no husband to make her way in this city, especially if she had a family to take care of.

"So Peter Morley is the man who's making the poteen?" I said. "What a strange world it is."

"He calls himself James Francis, since he left your friend Rose," Aloysius said. "But yes, this James Francis is the same man, and he's a very talented distiller. I've sent some men to bring him to me at a location in the wilds of Delaware. I'll be needing to leave now to meet them, so we must wrap things up here, Mary."

"What role do I play in this?" I said.

"Why, the same role you've always played," he said. "You put the word out among your friends that you have some new merchandise on offer. In fact, I want you to give them a sample or two, just so they can see how special it is. Then, when the orders come in, you pass them along to me."

He pushed his chair back and stood up. "Well, it's been nice chatting with you, Mary, but I must leave for my meeting with your friend Peter."

I stood up also. "Give my regards to him. I have no love for the man, but I feel sorry for Rose, getting mixed up with a scoundrel like that. I have a grudge against her, but I wouldn't wish him on my worst enemy."

"Oh, Rose is managing," he said. "Not without trouble, of course -- we all have our dose of that, don't we? Of her three boys, one has done well for himself. He's on the rise in his company, a printing outfit in West Philadelphia. One of her sons died, and the other is addicted to drink and will surely drink himself to death in a few years. Rose herself is married to another man -- his name is Martin Lancaster."

Once again, I gasped in shock. Martin Lancaster, the son of the family Rose and I worked for so many years ago! A rich man, to be sure. I knew from the start he was fond of Rose, but I never thought they'd end up married. People from his social class didn't marry girls like Rose.

"I expect she has a grand life, then," I said. "The Lancasters were wealthy people."

"Not anymore," Aloysius said. "The father died a few years ago and they never recovered. The Lancasters had their problems. Martin has a modest income as a criminal lawyer -- he's defended a few associates of mine, as it happens -- but he and Rose are far from wealthy."

"Where do they live?" I asked.

"Why, over in Kensington," he said. "In a little house. Rose has a job as a saleslady at the Wanamakers department store. You should visit her sometime, Mary," he said, laughing. "I'm sure you'd have lots to talk about. You've both come quite far from Skibbereen, haven't you?"

103

"That we have," I said. "But I have no wish to talk to Rose Sullivan Morley, after what she did to me. I don't forget when I'm wronged, Aloysius."

He grinned broadly. "Spoken like a true Irishwoman, Mary. We carry our grudges for many a year, don't we? We have long memories. Well, I'll be saying goodbye to you, for I've some business to arrange between myself and your gentleman friend, Mr. Morley."

He smiled, and it sent a chill through me. I knew it would not go well for James, or Peter as he was known to me, if he did not cooperate.

For it was a fact that Aloysius always got his way.

I went home from that meeting with my head crowded with thoughts. I was amazed that Peter Morley, or James Francis, as he was now calling himself, was still around, and that he created a new life for himself. I felt sorry for Rose, that he'd wronged her so badly, leaving her with three children. I had carried a grudge for years about what Rose had done to me, and now I felt myself softening towards her. She'd made a mistake getting mixed up with that rascal, no doubt about that.

But now she'd married, and to Martin Lancaster, of all people. I remembered the way he used to moon about Rose so many years ago. I used to tease Rose about it, that our employer's son was in love with her, and she'd get red in the face and tell me to shut my mouth. She was embarrassed, but we both knew he had feelings for her. Rose only had eyes for that handsome Peter Morley, though, and she made the wrong choice with her heart.

But that's what so many of us do, don't we? The very same thing happened to me, in the matter of Aloysius Declan O'Toole. He was as poisonous to me as the bite of a rattlesnake, but I lost my heart to him nonetheless. I don't know why these things happen; it must be some perversity about us women, that we choose the man who's worst for us, and go into it with our eyes open.

And yet, some of us are lucky enough to find a man who loves us in the way Francis Dillon loved me, and maybe that's what Rose had with Martin Lancaster. A man who will bandage up your wounds and stroke your hair and love the person inside of you, and who does it in a selfless way, seeking nothing for himself.

I was thankful for what I had with Francis. He and I had settled into what I called an October romance, where it was pleasant to just be in each other's company, reaping the harvest of our years in peace. Francis didn't put on his work clothes much anymore; he ran his business from an office now, and he had meetings with powerful people, usually with me at his side, and we talked of costs and estimates and projections all the time now.

But every night we'd sit on the porch of our big house in the suburbs and look at the rolling, sloping grounds and the garden with the little fish pond in it, and we'd watch the sun go down over the trees. Francis would turn to me and say, "Ah, Mary, I still can't believe what a lucky man I am," and each time it gave me a thrill. He was a fine, decent man, and he loved me very much, and if I never had that other feeling, the one where you have a fire inside that can only be quenched by the touch of another's skin, well, what of it? I preferred to spend my nights on that porch watching the sunset with him, and no other man on this Earth. I wanted Francis Dillon next to me in bed, not Aloysius O'Toole.

But there was one man I did want to see, and that was Peter Morley. I had a curiosity about him that would not be satisfied until I laid eyes on him again. I had to see him, and so one day I asked Dooley McCourt to take me to meet him.

"I'm picking up an order of moonshine tomorrow night," he said. "If you want to come with me, Mrs. Dillon, I'll take you along. Mr. O'Toole has set him up in a farmhouse in Delaware, and that's where he makes the stuff."

It was lucky for me that Dillon Brickwork had expanded now into nearby dioceses, and Francis was down in Baltimore for the next few days supervising some new schools that were being built there. I could go to Delaware without attracting suspicion from Francis.

We drove for what seemed like hours through the wilds of Delaware, passing miles of farms surrounded by woodlands, and with here and there a miserable little town with a white clapboard church, a filling station, and not much else to merit the name. Finally we turned off the main road and drove a long way down a rutted dirt road, and came to a greasy little house hidden by some trees and scrubby bushes, and it reeked of potatoes and alcohol.

There was a skinny, sour-faced young man sitting on the porch, and he looked at me with narrowed eyes when I got out of the truck.

"Who are you?" he said.

"My name's Mary Driscoll," I said. "I'm here to see James Francis."

The skinny man glanced at Dooley, who said, "It's all right, Tim. She works for Mr. O'Toole."

He thought that over for a moment, then stood up and snarled, "Wait here." He went through the door, and in a moment, a tall man came out on the porch. He had white hair, and his face was scored by many lines, but he was still handsome. It was Peter Morley, in the flesh.

"I'm told you want to speak with me," he said, peering at me as if he didn't recognize me. "Is there something I can do for you?"

"Why, Peter Morley," I said. "Do you not remember me, Mary Driscoll? The years haven't changed me that much, have they?

CHAPTER FIFTEEN

Peter Morley blinked once or twice, and I saw his face redden at the mention of his old name, but then the light of recognition shone in his eyes.

"Is it Mary?" he said. "Sorry I am I did not recognize you, Mary. My eyes don't work as well as they used to, I am afraid."

He came down off the porch and put his hand on my shoulder. "It's good to see you, Mary. Will you come inside and sit for awhile?"

"No, I will not," I said. "'Tis a gorgeous fall day, Peter, and it looks like lovely country out here. Why don't we take a walk? We could chat a while as we walk." I had no intention of going inside that house. I wanted to be far away from the hungry ears of Dooley McCourt, who I suspected would report back to Aloysius anything he heard me say. Besides, I didn't like the look of that sour-faced man on the porch. He seemed to hold a grudge against the world, the kind of man who thought it his duty to take issue with anything a person said.

Peter seemed surprised, but then he said, "Ah, I suppose I can spare a few minutes to be out in the sunshine on such a glorious day." He turned to the man on the porch. "Tim, go watch the works for me, will you? Watch the temperature on the cooker doesn't get too high. I won't be long." The sour-faced man went inside without a word.

We started down a dirt path between rows of corn taller than Peter. The breeze rustled through the leaves as we walked along, and the sun was warm on my skin.

"It must be twenty five years since I've laid eyes on you, Mary," he said, finally.

"'Tis near thirty," I said.

"Is it that long?" he said. "The time goes by so fast. It seems like only yesterday we were young and full of spirit. I remember feeling like I had the whole world in front of me back then. I lost that somewhere along the way."

"Was that when you left Rose and changed your name?" I said.

His face clouded. "Ah, Mary, that is a sore subject you're bringing up. I am not proud of it, but 'tis true I left her. It was a bad time, and I felt like I was drowning. Do you remember the Panic of 1893? Everyone was out of work. Rose and I had three small boys, living on my wages, and I was worried night and day that I'd lose my position. I didn't handle it well, I'm ashamed to say. I dreamed about a fresh start, a new life where I could leave all my troubles behind. I met a woman, a lovely English lass, and she made me happy again, after so many years of trouble and woe. It was the coward's way out, I admit, but I left my old life behind and started a new one."

"And how has your life been with that wife?" I said.

His face darkened again. "I have trouble there as well, Mary. She left me, nearly ten years ago now. She found I was seeing another woman."

"Lord, you are quite the faithless man," I exclaimed. "I don't expect much from any man, but you're in a class by yourself, Peter Morley."

"I am weak when it comes to women, I admit," he said. He winked and said, "You know that very well, Mary."

It was the first time he'd made reference to the night we'd spent together so many years ago, and it made me stop in my tracks. I felt as if I'd had a heavy blow to the stomach, and I gasped for breath. To see him wink as if it were a trifling affair, no more important than a ride on a roller coaster at a carnival, why, it made me sick. And to think a man like that had fathered my Luke! It was enough to get my blood boiling. I wouldn't tell him about the boy -- I'd never let him know he had another child in this world, but I wasn't going to let him get away with that smirk on his face.

I slapped him across the cheek. I hit him so hard my hand hurt, and I saw an ugly red welt appear on his handsome face. His eyes looked stunned, and they blinked once or twice before he got control of himself.

"Why did you do that?" he said, rubbing his face.

"It's something I've wanted to do for a long time," I answered. "And happy I am that I lived long enough to get the chance to do it. You're nothing but a false and shallow man, Peter Morley, or whatever you call yourself now, and I hope you suffer for your sins."

He sighed, and his face suddenly looked very sad.

"I am suffering now, Mary," he said. "I know I've sinned, and I'm paying for it dearly. For the wrongs I did to Rose, I've only to look at that boy back in the house, my Tim. He's ruined his life with drink, and he blames me for it. I see it in his eyes, he's in Hell every day, and it's all my fault. And for the sins I did to Edith, I've lost her love, whom I thought I would spend my life with. I'm no more than a prisoner of this Aloysius O'Toole, all because I have so few choices now. I was living in a little room in Philadelphia with Tim, with barely enough to eat, and no work. I'm an old man, Mary, and I've got little time left. I had no choice but to come out here and work for this O'Toole fellow, making my poteen and hiding from the law in this godforsaken place. It's not the way I thought I'd live at the end of my mortal days."

He looked miserable, and a wave of pity for him came over me. I felt sorry that he'd come to this pass, and well I knew that he was in a bad place, if he were working for Aloysius.

"Watch yourself, Peter," I said. "I've known O'Toole for many a year, and he's a dangerous man. You'd do well to watch your step around him."

"Now, that's good advice," came a voice from behind us. "I'd listen to her carefully, Mr. Morley. Mary knows what she's talking about, don't you, Mary?"

It was O'Toole, and he was standing not ten feet behind us. He was wearing a long brown fur-trimmed Chesterfield coat and a bowler hat, looking for all the world like a banker or a lawyer. His gold tooth gleamed in the October sun. I was amazed that he'd come so close to us without making a sound. The corn waved in the breeze all around us, but apparently he'd walked through it without making any noise.

"You're like God himself, Aloysius," I said. "You appear and disappear whenever you wish. Or should I say the Devil himself?"

He laughed. "Call me what you will, Mary, it matters not to me. I have my ways, but I don't explain them. It's better to keep people guessing. So, I see you two have met. I got wind that you

111

were coming out here, Mary, and I decided to come and see just why you'd want to pay a visit to my distilling operation. Now what is the attraction, may I ask? Did you fancy a visit with your old friend Peter?"

I felt myself redden in the face, and my fists clenched at my sides. "I know what you're suggesting, O'Toole, and I resent it. I have my reasons for coming here, and you're not privy to them."

"It is just a friendly visit, Mr. O'Toole," Peter said. His voice betrayed his nervousness, and he was shuffling from one foot to the other as he spoke.

"I'm sure it is," Aloysius said, clasping his gloved hands behind his back. "It's very convenient for me that you're both here, however. I have a business proposition you'll both be interested in, and we might as well talk about it now."

"Here?" I said. "In the middle of a cornfield?"

"Why yes," he said. He put his finger on the end of his nose and winked. "In my line of work, it's a good policy not to discuss business when there are too many ears around." He jerked his thumb in the direction of the house. "I like privacy, and this is as private a place as any. I'll get right to the point: I'm going to expand my business to include a drinking establishment. I want you to supply the liquor, Mr. Morley, and I want you to run the place for me, Mrs. Dillon."

"Now you've surely gone mad," I said. "You're talking of running a speakeasy, of course. It's an illegal venture, and I'll not be a part of it. I'm too old to be thrown in jail for one of your schemes."

"And I can't make that much poteen," Peter said. "I'm barely able to keep up now. I'd need a bigger operation."

"Indeed you would," Aloysius said. "And I'll set you up with everything you need, my boy. Money's no object -- I'll buy the ingredients, the equipment, and the people. And you needn't worry about getting arrested, Mary. The police will turn a blind eye to the whole operation, I'll see to it. You must know I would take care of a detail like that."

"I know you think of everything," I said. "But I'm still not interested. I've done enough bad things for you, Aloysius O'Toole. I've been the instrument of your evil far too many times over the years. I'll not take this step, and put another stain on my soul. I reject your offer."

He smiled, and I saw the icy look come into his eyes. "Now, Mary, I wish you'd listen to reason. You see, you really have no choice. I have only to say the word and my Italian associates will make things very bad for your husband. I know you've spent a long time building up his business, and it would be a shame to see it all taken away from you. Why, you'd lose your big house, Mary! And that grand life you lead, going to all the parties with the high and mighty people? That would end too, I'm afraid. It would be terrible to see you go back to the kind of scuffling life you led thirty years ago, as if all your good fortune had been nothing but a dream."

His words made me shiver, and I wanted to run through the corn and get away from him. But there was nowhere to go, unless I took a boat back to Ireland, and that was out of the question.

I spat on the ground and said, "You're a bastard, Aloysius, and I rue the day I ever met you."

"Why, Mary," he said, spreading his arms wide. "I have only happy memories of our time together, and I'm sad that you do not. Be that as it may, I can see that I've convinced you of the wisdom of my line of reasoning. I am opening an establishment in Philadelphia within the month, and you will manage it for me. And you, Mr. Morley, will supply the best liquor on the east coast of this fair country."

"Within a month!" Peter said. "That's impossible. I can't make more than a few cases of the stuff by then. What you're asking can't be done, man!"

Aloysius smiled again, and rubbed his hands. "Mr. Morley doesn't know me very well, does he, Mary? I've promised a lot of people I'm opening a first-rate speakeasy soon, and I don't make promises I can't keep. I'll get you everything you need to supply me with your excellent liquor, my good man. And you will make it for me, or that miserable son of yours back at the house will pay the price. Do you understand?"

"Yes," Peter said, wearily. "I understand."

"Good," Aloysius said, rubbing his gloved hands together. "Now, let's get back to the house, shall we? This air is a bit too cold for my liking. I think winter is coming, and it reminds me of the dark, bleak winters of my youth in Dublin. I'd much rather think of more pleasant things, like how much money we'll all make, my friends."

He turned and strode back to the house, knowing that we would follow him.

So, God preserve me, at the age of 65 I became the proprietress of a speakeasy. Me, Mary Driscoll, who'd worked so

114

hard to become the soul of respectability. Why, I was married to a man who owned a successful business building schools for the church, and I socialized with the high and mighty, having afternoon teas at my house with the wives of the most respectable men in town.

Now I was going to have two lives, and I knew it would not be easy to manage them both.

The first thing I had to do was come to an understanding with Francis Dillon. I sat him down and said, "I won't lie to you, Francis, and I won't go sneaking around behind your back. There's something you have to know, and I'm going to come right out with it. I need you to keep silent, for it's a long story, and I must tell it to you all the way through before I stop."

I went into the whole sordid tale about Aloysius and Peter (although I never told him about my boy Luke), and how I'd been helping Aloysius find customers for his bootlegging operation, and now things were taking a giant step further, with the opening of the speakeasy. I told him that Aloysius was forcing me to do it, and I had no choice.

"I won't have you doing this," he said, his face reddening while he sat with his hands clenched on his lap, as if he wanted to hit someone. "It's wrong. You know yourself I don't touch a drop of liquor, Mary, I never have. I won't be a party to this plan, and I won't have you in on it either. I'll go talk to this man Aloysius, and I'll tell him you're not doing it. It's illegal, and dangerous, and I won't have you risking harm to yourself."

I smiled at him and touched his arm. "I thank you for your concern, Francis, but you won't get anywhere talking to Aloysius O'Toole. He's a hard, cold man, and he'll not deal with you kindly. I know him well, and you'll be a marked man if you cross him. I told you he's the one who took care of your problem with those gangsters. You know they've never been back -- it's because of Aloysius, that's how powerful he is. It's for you I'm doing this, man. I don't want you hurt in any way, and he can hurt you badly."

He was sitting on a sofa across from me, but he came over and knelt at my feet, and took my hand in his.

"Mary, I have had more happiness in these years with you than I ever dreamed possible. I don't ever want it to end. However, I can't let this man rule our lives like this. He's evil, that's what he is, and I won't let him scare me."

"Then be afraid for me," I said, gripping his hand. I'm not one for crying, but I could not stop the tears, when I thought of this good man being killed. "I couldn't live without you, Francis, that's the God's honest truth. You're the only person who's ever really loved me, and I couldn't bear to be without you. Please, please, do as I ask. You must let me do what I need to do for Aloysius, and let it be. It will be like a room you don't go in, or a door you never knock on. Just keep what I do separate, then you'll never have to bother your conscience about it. Please, I beg of you, Francis!"

He wiped my tears away and said, "As you wish, Mary. I don't like it, but I will do as you want. I'll ask no questions, and I'll let you do what you must do."

It was a strange way for a husband and wife to live, I admit, but I had to keep a wall between the two parts of my life.

CHAPTER SIXTEEN

There were two Mary Driscolls now.

One Mary Driscoll continued to be a pillar of the church, organizing committees and hosting dinners, hobnobbing with the clergy and the rich donors. The other Mary Driscoll operated a speakeasy, where for a price you could buy a bottle of bootleg whiskey, listen to some hot jazz, and play dice or cards at tables in a back room.

The place was nothing special, just three rooms on the first floor of a building downtown that had an entrance off a cobblestoned alleyway. It was open on Friday and Saturday nights, and you had to give a password to a big Irishman named Fergus before he'd let you in. Inside, there was a large room with a bar, and a small stage with tables in front of it. I always had entertainment. The jazz musicians who were passing through town would stop in and play for a few sets, and you never knew who you'd see sitting on the rickety wooden chairs on the stage -- sometimes we had big names, like Bix Beiderbecke, Bing Crosby, James P. Johnson, or Sidney Bechet, and other nights it was a collection of unknowns. There were a couple of bathrooms, and a small kitchen where I had a cook who could make a few dishes, and then there was the back room where the gamblers went. Aloysius paid off the police so they left us alone, but every once in awhile they had to raid the place just to make things look good. They always tipped us off before they came, and I made sure I was never there. There was a false wall in the gamblers' room that led to a set of stairs and a basement passage to an outside exit, just so the high rollers could get away before the Paddy wagon showed up.

I was always the first to leave whenever we got the word; it wouldn't do for my standing in the community to spend a night in jail.

It was quite a life, and there were times when I wondered at the sanity of it all. It was hard to keep my head on straight with all the roles I was playing, but I tried to always be myself, no matter what. There was a need for a level head among all this rowdiness, and I was the woman for that.

The speakeasy was like a playground for grownups; it had everything they needed to forget the world for a few hours. They could be different than they were in the daytime; let their hair down, so to speak, and it was always a shock to me to see a judge or politician come in looking like he'd never smiled a day in his life, and by the end of the night he'd be roaring with laughter and dancing the Charleston with some pretty young thing.

And it wasn't just judges who let their hair down. There were plenty of fine, upstanding representatives of the religious community who came through our door on Saturday nights, and I am sure they had a lot to repent for the next morning.

I could usually spot them, the priests and parsons, for they always showed up with a guilty look on their faces and tried to stay in the shadows at first. After they got a few belts of whiskey in them, they'd loosen up and have a good time, but they always seemed to be hiding something, and I knew what it was. They didn't want to be recognized, and if they were, most of them didn't come back.

However, some came back anyway, depending on the fraternity of sinners in my joint to keep their secret. There was one like that, hardly more than a boy, it seemed, who I remember well.

He had a shock of strawberry blonde hair, freckles, and the look about him of a farm boy from upstate. He skulked in one Saturday night with his coat collar turned up, and a hat pulled low on his head, and he sat at the bar drinking by himself for awhile. He didn't say much, and it was clear he didn't want to be recognized. He had sad eyes, though, and I felt sorry for him. I sent a girl named Florence over to talk to him. She was a cute young thing herself, about the same age as himself, and she was as bubbly as a new glass of champagne, with not a thought in her head. She was supposed to wait on the customers, and she had to keep busy, but I told her to stop by and chat with him whenever she was able.

So I suppose I'm to blame for what happened between them. He called himself John Wilkins, and told Florence he was an editor for the Farm Journal, which was headquartered in the Curtis Publishing building on Washington Square. He seemed an educated man, and he spoke well, but there was something innocent and unworldly about him. Florence called him Willy, and she fell for him instantly. It was clear he felt the same way for her.

Before long she was telling me that he was writing poetry to her, and telling her she was the only woman he ever loved. Normally I would laugh at such nonsense from a man, but something about this fellow made me think it was true. It got so he'd stay long after closing time, and they'd sit at a table in a corner and look into each other's eyes and kiss and generally do all the things you do the first time you fall in love.

I thought they were a charming couple, and maybe that's what made me let down my guard. Normally I would have discouraged the girls on my staff from getting involved with customers, but for once I didn't, and I regretted it later.

119

For there came a day when a priest showed up in his full clerical garb at my door. I was there on a Saturday afternoon getting things ready for that night's business, and Fergus came to me as I stood behind the bar making note of what supplies needed to be restocked.

"There's a priest at the door," he said. "He wants to come in."

"Tell him we're not open," I said. "He can come back in two hours when we're open for business."

"He's not here for entertainment," Fergus said. "He looks plenty mad, and he's demanding to speak to the manager of this 'place of sin'. He won't listen to reason, Mary. I think you should come and talk to him."

I put down my pad and pencil, and went out to the door.

"We're not open for business," I said, through the peephole. "Come back in two hours."

"I'm not here to patronize your business," the man said. "I demand to speak to the proprietor. It's a matter of urgent concern, and I will not go away till I've spoken to him."

"All right, I'll speak to you in the alley," I said. I was afraid he was one of these holy rollers who'd be offended by what he saw of Aloysius's drinking establishment, and I didn't want to give him any fuel for his sermon tomorrow morning. I could see him staring out at his congregation and bellowing, "Why, they have row upon row of bottles, just stacked behind the bar, for anyone to drink!". No, I wasn't going to have any of that, so I decided it would be safer to speak to him in the alley.

I opened the door and came out to the alley, and he stood there looking at me sternly, with his hands on his hips. He was about six feet tall, with a fine head of black wavy hair, and bushy dark eyebrows. He looked to be about 35 years old. He was a priest, that was clear as day, dressed in his black cassock, with a black biretta on his head.

"Who are you?" he said, glaring at me.

"My name is Mary," I said. "I'm the person who runs this place."

"You?" he said, raising his eyebrows. "A woman?"

"Yes I am a woman," I said. "And what of it?"

"I am shocked that a woman would run a place like this," he said. "It's scandalous, just scandalous. Have you no decency?"

I sighed. "Father, I would appreciate it if you'd spare me the sermon. I'm sure you have plenty of thoughts on this matter, but I have a lot to do before we open tonight. Is there something in particular you wanted to talk about? And who, by the way, am I talking to?"

He pursed his lips, reddening, and seemed to be deciding if he wanted to call down fire and brimstone on my head. Gradually, though, he calmed himself and said, "My name is Father Lorcan Boone, pastor of Sacred Heart of Jesus parish, and yes, as a matter of fact, there is something I want to talk to you about. You have a customer of this, this -- establishment -- named James Wilkins, who has been led astray by one of your girls. I am here to talk about this situation, and what needs to be done about it."

121

"It's that, is it?" I said. "Well, I'm not a nursemaid, Father, just a businesswoman. I don't get involved in the personal lives of my customers. I'm afraid I can't help you in that regard."

His face reddened again, and he exploded. "But he's a priest, woman! He's a priest of God, and he's having relations with one of your girls!"

I shrugged my shoulders, which I am sure was shocking to him. I'm ashamed to say it, but it's true that his revelation didn't make a whit of difference to me.

"And what of it?" I said. "I've been in this world more than 60 years, Father, and I've seen a lot of things in my time. If you're of a mind that I should be shocked or get myself worked up about it, well, that's not going to happen. Your Father James is no different than others I've seen who have visited this place. It doesn't surprise me, to be honest, seeing as how your outfit thinks it's a fine thing to cut a man off from his natural urges. The poor fellows sometimes look so lonesome I feel sorry for them."

His eyes blazed with fury, and he was all a tremble as he said, "I've heard blasphemy in my day, but never from the lips of a woman -- and you an Irishwoman, to boot! You should be ashamed of yourself, questioning the doctrines of Holy Mother Church. Were you not raised Catholic in Ireland? How can you say such things without blushing?"

"I'll say whatever I want," I retorted. "It's a free country, if you haven't noticed. And I'm only saying what's true, anyway. I've spent more time around priests than even yourself, I'll wager. I know what a hardship it is to them to go without a woman's touch. And for what? I thought Jesus came into the world to make love prosper, not to stifle it. The Pope ought to change that policy."

"The Pope isn't going to take advice from the proprietor of a speakeasy, and neither am I," he said, through gritted teeth. "The fact remains that Father James, who is my assistant at Sacred Heart parish not a mile distant from here, has fallen in love with one of your serving girls. I want this relationship ended now. You must fire that girl, and instruct your doorkeeper not to let Father James on your premises anymore."

"I can't do it, and I won't do it," I said, putting my hands on my hips. "There's no way you can make me, Father."

His chin stuck out with fury. "I'll see that you're closed down," he said. "You won't last another week."

I stuck my own chin out. "Good luck. The man behind this establishment has friends in very high places, Father. I don't care who you know; they're not as powerful as the people he knows. You'll be running into a brick wall."

He threw his hands up in frustration. "Don't you understand this is serious, woman? This is an immortal soul we're talking about! He's hardly more than a boy; he came straight from the family farm to the seminary. He has no experience with the ways of the world, and he's had his head turned by a pretty girl. He could be a good priest, but this will ruin him."

I was not going to be moved. "I told you, I am not his nursemaid. If he's fallen in love with the girl, maybe he wasn't meant to be a priest."

"He's breaking his vows!" the priest said.

"And that's his decision, not mine," I answered. "Now, if you'll excuse me, Father, I have business to attend to."

I rapped on the door, and Fergus opened it. I stood in the doorway. "Goodbye, Father," I said. "I hope things go well for your young priest friend."

He turned on his heel and stalked down the alley, but not before saying, "Things will not go well. Mark my words, they will not go well."

CHAPTER SEVENTEEN

I gave it no more thought until later that day, when Florence came to work. I took her aside and said, "Did you know your gentleman friend is a priest?"

"Yes," she said, giggling. "I knew that. Why?"

"Because his pastor came to see me today. He's very concerned that the young Father is making a big mistake by falling in love with you. You have to be gentle with a boy like that, Florence. He has no experience with women."

She giggled again. "Oh, don't worry about that, Mary. I'm done with him anyway. There's a rich banker named Mr. Jessup that sends me flowers. I met him one night when James wasn't here. Mr. Jessup tells me I could be on the stage. He's going to get me dancing lessons. I'm sweet on him now."

"Have you told James?" I said. "I don't think he'll like it."

She screwed her pretty face into a frown. "Aw, he'll get over it. We had some laughs for a while, but it's over, and that's all she wrote. I'm going to give him the lowdown tonight."

I told myself I couldn't worry about the problems of a lovesick young man, and I tried to put it out of my mind. I was too busy, and that was the end of it.

It was a typical Saturday night, with a lot of noise, laughter, a fight or two that Fergus had to break up, and general merriment. I didn't notice that the young priest was even in attendance, until towards closing time, when we were shooing the customers out the door, and I saw him sitting at a table with Florence. She had her serious look on, screwing up her forehead and squinting, and she was holding his hand while she gave him the bad news. I saw him mouth the word, "No!", and then he stood up and ran out of the room blindly, knocking chairs over on the way.

Florence didn't give it a second thought. She finished cleaning up as if nothing had happened, trilling a song in her little girl voice. When she left, her new beau Jessup was waiting for her at the door with a bouquet of flowers. She gave him a big kiss and they went on their way, nuzzling each other like two lovebirds.

I didn't think of the priest for a week, but the next Saturday Fergus came to tell me that "the Father from last week is back". I sighed and went to the door, and stepped out into the alley to see Father Boone standing there with a look of weary sadness on his handsome face.

The sky was gray and it was spitting cold rain, and I motioned for him to come in out of the rain. He shook his head no.

"I came to tell you that Father Wilkins killed himself yesterday," he said. "He left a note that said it was because of the woman he met here. He thought he was in love with her, and she rejected him. He hung himself in his room."

I felt the strength go out of my legs, and I had to lean against the wall to steady myself.

"Killed himself?" I said. "Over a girl like Florence? Why?"

He frowned. "I told you before, he was just a boy. He had no idea about women. I'm sure he'd never even kissed one before. He lost his head, is all."

"I didn't know it would come to this," I said.

"Well, it did," he snapped. "And now he can't be buried in the Church, because of the mortal sin on his soul. Suicide is a grave sin, in case you didn't know."

"But he was just a boy," I said. "You can't judge him like that. Many men fall in love foolishly. It's just a passing thing, and they get over it. If he had had someone to talk sense into him, he'd still be here. It was just a rash impulse he followed. How can you know what was going through his head?"

He sighed, and his face suddenly looked older, world weary. "I don't make these rules, Mary. The Church in her wisdom says that to take one's life is a grave sin. It means he died without confessing his sin and receiving absolution for it. That's a serious matter."

"I'll never understand these confounded rules," I said. "They're designed to drive a person crazy, that's what it seems to me."

"I'm not here to have a discussion about theology with you," he said. "I came to tell you what happened, and to let you know that I'm going to say a few prayers over his coffin tonight, at the funeral home. His parents are coming on the noon train tomorrow to take the body back home. He'll be buried in a non-Catholic cemetery. I'll be saying prayers at 7:00 this evening, at the Donovan Funeral Home on 12th Street near Locust. You may come if you wish."

He turned on his heel and left, and I listened to the sound of his shoes clattering on the cobblestone alley for a minute, then I composed myself and went inside.

127

Of course I was going to go. I wanted to pay my respects, and to say a prayer or two myself.

That night when Florence came to work, I told her what had happened. A cloud of concern crossed her pretty face, but it was gone as fast as a summer shower. "I'm sorry to hear that," she trilled. "He was a nice man. Mr. Jessup took me to the best place for dinner last night!" It was apparent she would never give another thought to James Wilkins for the rest of her life.

When I went to the funeral home, I found it was a brick building that could have been just another row house except for the neat little sign out front that said, "Donovan Funeral Services" in white letters on a black background. Inside, there were rooms tastefully decorated, and a serious man in a black suit who introduced himself as Mr. Brendan Donovan escorted me to one of the rooms, where I found Father Boone. There was a plain wooden casket at one end of the room, with rows of chairs surrounding it. The chairs were empty.

"I'm glad to see you, Mary," the priest said. He folded his arms across his chest and looked down at the casket.

"Why is it closed?" I said. "I thought caskets were always open."

"I told you he hung himself," Father Boone said. "His face was contorted in a horrible mask when I found him. They couldn't do anything to make him look better, I'm afraid."

He opened a black prayerbook and started to recite a few prayers, asking God's forgiveness for this terrible sin James Wilkins had committed. I prayed along, mouthing the prayers with him, but inside I was saying a different prayer.

128

Why is it, God, that you let a boy like that get himself into such a fix? Why take him away from his family and the life he knew, and bring him to the big city where he could meet a girl like Florence, who cared not a whit for him? He was nothing but a handsome face to her, someone who would tell her how pretty she was. Why did you throw him into that mess? And, when he saw no way out of this unrequited love, and he took the only path he saw open to him, why do you now turn your back on him? What sense is there in that? Why do you let us make such fools of ourselves? Why did you give me a child and then take it away, so that I'd spend my life in pain, wondering where he ended up and what became of him? Why, why, why?

When Father Boone was finished, he made the sign of the Cross and said, "Amen". There was a silence between us for a minute, as he laid his hand on the wood of the casket, and then he said, "I must be going. I have work to do back at the parish."

"Father," I said, on an impulse. "I was thinking of taking a walk down by the river, just to clear my head. It's a pretty night, and I like to look at the waterfront on a night like this. Would you care to join me?"

"Thank you, but I should be getting back," he said. Then, he seemed to sag a bit, and he said, "But maybe a walk would do me good. I could spare a few minutes, I suppose."

And so we left the funeral home and walked down Locust Street, then up to Market and down to the waterfront. It was a glorious night, with stars winking on here and there, and the sound of men unloading boats, cars passing over the new Ben Franklin Bridge to New Jersey, and the water lapping at the piers.

"It's a strange life, isn't it, Father?" I said. "All the people in this city, rushing about in the grip of their plans and dreams. I'm not a woman for dwelling in the past, but this puts me in mind of the River Ilen that ran through the town of Skibbereen, where I grew up. I used to go to a quiet spot on the riverbank when I was a girl of 14 and kiss a boy named Brendan Corgan. That was the most important thing in my life back then. Life was less complicated, I suppose."

"When did you come to America?" he asked.

"Nearly 40 years ago," I said. "I was just a girl when I came over. I'd never seen so many people. I was entranced by it -- I thought I'd gone to Heaven, I did."

He laughed. "I wouldn't use the word 'Heaven' to describe this city. There's a lot of poverty, sickness, and cruelty here. I don't associate those things with Heaven."

"Right you are," I said. "Although I didn't see all of that in the beginning. It's only with the passing of the years that I saw the grime beneath the surface of things. And what about you? Where do you come from?"

"A home in Bryn Mawr, on the Main Line," he said. "I grew up in a big house with plenty of material things. It wasn't enough for me. I was dissatisfied with that life, and I went searching for an answer to why I felt so empty inside. I found it in the Church."

"So you gave up the comforts of a life on the Main Line to come down here and serve the poor?" I said. "I wouldn't mind taking your old life, Father, no offense to the path you've chosen."

He laughed. "It has its challenges, this life, but I've learned a lot about the human soul, and it never ceases to amaze me."

"I'm sure you're right, Father," I said. "We're all strange creatures. We'll rob you with one hand and bless you with the other. What a crazy lot we are."

There was the sound of a tugboat far down the river, and the priest paused, then said, "Do you know the biggest lesson I've learned? That people are never really here. They're always planning for the future, scheming and praying and brooding about it, even on their deathbed. They think things will be better tomorrow, next week, next year. They don't trust in God to take care of things, and just live their lives. That's all it is, you know -- just trust in God, and stop worrying about the next thing that's coming along."

"Where is your parish, Father?" I said.

"On 3rd Street in Southwark," he said. "It's mostly poor Irish families. Cardinal Dougherty has been trying to close down the ethnic parishes. It used to be you'd have an Italian church next to a German one, and across the street from an Irish one, and none of the faithful from one parish would set foot inside the other church. The Cardinal thinks we shouldn't have a situation like that. We're all believers in the same Redeemer. He's right, but old habits die hard. My parish is a holdout -- my people are dead set against closing the church."

"We Irish are stubborn souls, aren't we?" I said.

"To be sure," he said. "I have my hands full serving them. They struggle every day, the lot of them. There's none of this economic boom the newspapers talk about in my neighborhood. I see a lot of people who can't pay their rent."

"There's plenty of money being made," I said. "I see it in the world I live in, but sometimes I wonder if the bubble will burst. I know shoeshine boys who play the stock market, Father. That doesn't seem like a proper thing to me. Something's got to give."

He shrugged. "Well, maybe so, Mary. But it won't be my worry. I have higher concerns than making money."

"You can have your higher concerns," I said. "I'll still take the money. I know it's not what Jesus preached, but it makes me feel better at night to know I've got a few dollars put away. But I do like to use it for a good end now and then. What is it you need, Father? Do you need repairs at your church? Perhaps new clothes for some of the poor children? A new altar cloth? Just tell me, and I'll give you the money for it."

The tugboat was getting closer, and its horn was louder.

He frowned. "I couldn't take your money, Mary. I don't approve of how you're making it. It's dirty money, and I'll have no part of it."

I felt the anger rise to my face. "So you'd deny some poor soul a new pair of pants because of your scruples, would you? I think you should be ashamed to hear yourself speak those words. Money is money, no matter how it's made, and if it can be put to good use, I say why not do it? I know you could use it, man. Why, you've got holes in your shoes and your pants are so shiny I can see my reflection in them. It's just blind stubbornness to say no to me when I'm offering you money you could use."

"I'll not take it," he said, sticking his chin out, "and that's my final word on it." He turned and bowed stiffly to me. "It's been a nice half hour chatting with you, Mary, but I must be going. There's a sick child I must stop in to see, and an old man who may die tonight, so I have to give him Last Rites. God be with you, Mary.

You are welcome to come to Mass at Sacred Heart of Jesus anytime."

He bowed again and strode off, and I thought how stupid and stubborn he was.

I will find a way to help him out, whether he wants the money or not.

CHAPTER EIGHTEEN

1929

There was a sort of madness in the air.

People were mad with money, drink, ambition, and a hunger to have more, more, more. The speakeasy was doing better than ever -- the place was packed with people every Friday and Saturday night, and O'Toole, knowing a good thing when he saw it, had started opening the place on Thursday nights too. Peter Morley's bootlegging operation in Delaware was five times the size it was when he started, and even then it was hard for him to keep up with the demand.

Sometimes Peter would take a break from his work and ride with the delivery truck on its rounds, and he'd come to visit with me before the speakeasy opened. He dressed very well these days, with a crease in his pants and a carnation in his lapel. He told me he had a stock portfolio, like just about everyone else in the world, it seemed, and he said his investments were doing well.

But I saw the haunted look in his eyes. He claimed he still hadn't reconciled with his second wife, the Englishwoman, and it was clear it hurt him to the core. "She'll let me come and visit once in awhile," he said. "But she won't allow me to stay the night. 'Tis a precious thing I've lost, Mary, and I'll never get it back." He was living in a rented room with Tim, his alcoholic son, and he said Tim's heath was failing. There was sadness about him, and he had the look of a frail old man to me.

O'Toole came around too, to collect his money. Sometimes he sent one of his goons, but at times he came himself. He had a full head of white hair now, and his eyes looked colder than ever. You'd think he'd be a happy man, with all the money he was making, but there was an edge of meanness to him these days. He rarely smiled, and he couldn't speak to you for five minutes without cutting you with his words. He brooked no opposition, and I saw grown men trembling in his presence if they had to say no to him -- they knew other men had come to a bad end when they crossed Aloysius O'Toole.

Every night when I closed the speakeasy and had my driver -- who was Dooley McCourt now -- take me home, I went in the house, no matter how late it was, and drew a bath for myself. I had to wash off all the dirt I felt on me from being around people like Aloysius. I wouldn't tell Francis a word about what went on in that place -- I didn't want to introduce the poison into our home.

I had to do more to make myself feel clean, so I found a way to give money to Father Boone. I learned he had a housekeeper/cook named Kitty Boyle, an old Irishwoman from Galway, and I followed her into the market one day when she was buying food for dinner.

I told her I wanted to give money in an envelope to Father Boone, once a month or so, but I didn't want him to know who was giving it. She was not to tell him, no matter what. She was to say she found the envelope inside the kitchen door when she opened it in the morning.

She looked at me like I was talking nonsense. "Why, I can't participate in that," she huffed. "You'd be asking me to lie to a priest, and I could never do such a thing. Why would you want to give money to the good father without him knowing who you are? It sounds suspicious to me."

"Have you never heard of the parable Jesus told about the Pharisees who make such a fuss when they give their money in the synagogue?" I said. "And then He gave the example of the poor old woman who gives her one coin, and does it quietly. I'm like that old woman, you see. God has blessed my husband's business, and I have a few extra coins I can use to help good Father Boone, but I want no credit for it. I prefer to do my charity in secret."

That won her over, quoting the Bible. She agreed at once, and I set it up that every month I'd drop off the envelope on the first Monday.

I knew that Father Boone would question her, but I trusted that she wouldn't tell him who I was.

It was the least I could do when I was making all this money, to give some of it back to the poor.

So once a month I got up with the milkmen and bakers, and I had Dooley McCourt take me down to the rectory, a two story brick building next to the little stone church on 3rd Street, and I slipped a plain envelope between the outside and inside doors to the kitchen. It made me feel good to think that my money was going to do some good in the world.

As the year of 1929 went on, there was a crazy energy in the air, and anyone could see there was trouble brewing. I bought no stock, and no bonds -- I didn't trust all this hysterical talk, and I kept my money in gold coins in a safe deposit box. I was having trouble sleeping, I had such presentiments of doom.

And then one day Peter Morley came to see me, and I knew from one look at him what he was about to do.

He wouldn't talk to me in the speakeasy, but we walked down to the Reading Terminal market and got a booth in the back of a small restaurant, ordering a lunch of fried oysters and tea.

"I'm getting out," he said. "I'll make no more liquor for Aloysius O'Toole."

"You can't get out," I said. "He's not the kind of man you can just say 'I quit', to. Nobody says that to him."

"I know," he said twisting his big hands as if he were washing dirt off them. "And that's why I went to the authorities. I've been meeting with a federal agent in Wilmington. They're going to raid the operation next week, when Aloysius is there. I've arranged to be away when it happens."

"Are you mad?" I said. "He'll find out your plan, and you'll be a dead man."

"It's a chance I have to take, Mary," he said. "I can't go on like this forever. Sure, I've made some money, but I'm living in fear of getting arrested. I can't go to jail at my age. I'll die there. Things have been getting better with my Edith, she's warming up to me at last, and I want to have a few good years with her before I die."

"Aloysius won't go quietly," I said. "He's capable of great violence. There will be blood shed."

"I well know it," Peter said. "It's a price that must be paid. If he chooses to fight, he will lose, God willing. The world will be rid of him, then. It would be better for us all, wouldn't it?"

"Do you think the world will be rid of evil just by getting rid of Aloysius O'Toole?" I said. "He's a powerful man, Peter, but he's only one man. His death will leave a space, and in time someone will fill it. As long as there's poverty in this world, there will be people who will stop at nothing to make money."

"What will you do, Mary?" Peter said. "Will you keep the place open after he's gone?"

"Not I," I said. "I'll lock the door and walk away from it. I've no wish to keep that place running. I'll go back to my Francis and try to forget these last few years. "

"'Tis a sorry world, isn't it?" Peter said, a look of great sadness in his eyes.

"Yes, but it's the only one we have," I said, "and we must make the best of it."

I saw Aloysius once more. He came in the place after closing on Friday night, and told me he'd not be in the next night, because he had some business to attend to in Delaware. I looked at him counting the money like a banker, gazing at the crisp notes with more love than he ever showed me, and I thought of how there was a time, years ago, when I would have felt sorry for him. But not now. There was no feeling except a wistfulness that all his riches weren't going to help him take one more breath tomorrow than God allowed him.

When the next day came, the stock market crashed. The newsboys were screaming the headlines on every street corner about the trouble on Wall Street. That night there was an air of mania about the patrons of our speakeasy. The men had scared looks in their eyes, and they drank with a manic energy. The women laughed louder, the musicians played with a frenzied pace, and the dancers clutched at each other like they were on the deck of a sinking ship.

I don't remember what time it was, perhaps 9:00, but of a sudden I got this shaking feeling and I had to sit down. I looked at the clock on the wall, and for a moment everything slowed down, and it was like I was in a bubble, with all the world moving in slow motion around me. It went on for an eternity of a minute, and then things speeded up again and I recovered.

But I knew at that moment Aloysius was dead.

When closing time came I emptied the till and counted out the pay for Fergus the doorman, plus the bartenders, the waitresses, and the men who ran the gambling tables in the back. I gave them all a bonus, and I said, "If I were in your shoes, I'd look to myself. There's change in the air, and I recommend you find other work. I'm leaving, and I know nothing of the future of this place."

When they all left I closed the door and locked it, and rode home and tried to forget the place as fast as I could.

When I got home I drew my bath as usual, and I took a good long soak in it. I was hoping to clean myself of all the grit and grime and stink of that place, and the evil of Aloysius O'Toole. He'd been a part of my life for almost 30 years, and the poison from him had leached into my soul. All I wanted now was to be rid of him, to dig him up like a weed and throw him away.

I was happy when I got out of the bath and put my nightgown on, for now I felt like I could finally give my whole heart and soul to Francis. He was a good man, and I'd grown to love him over the years, this faithful and true husband of mine. I had felt guilty that I couldn't love him like I loved Aloysius all those years ago, but now I was free to do so.

But something had happened in the years I'd run the speakeasy. Francis had become an old man, and I hadn't seen it. I looked at him in the bed, and I was shocked to see so many wrinkles in his face, so much white in his hair. His breathing was labored, and when he rolled over he winced, as if his body pained him.

I had been blind to what was happening right in front of me, because I was too caught up in the world of Aloysius O'Toole. I determined to do better, to treat Francis better now.

CHAPTER NINETEEN

Francis was slipping away from me. He moved more slowly, he had aches and pains in his joints, his eyes were failing, and he was always tired. There were times when he'd come home from work and hardly eat a bite of the dinner I prepared him. He'd go sit in his easy chair and turn on the radio, to listen to one of his favorite shows, but I'd find him with his head down, snoring after only five minutes.

He used to like to go with me to dinners and parties, or just to take a walk in the evenings, but sometimes now he'd say, "You go yourself, Mary. I'm a bit too tired tonight."

I wanted him to go to a doctor and get himself checked out, but he wouldn't.

"What can they do for me?" he'd say. "It's just all the years of hard work have taken their toll. I'm like an old dog who needs to rest more, that's all."

The years went on, and I could tell he wasn't keeping up with the business like he used to. There were problems with some of the men drinking on the jobs, and he didn't handle them like he did before. There were problems with jobs that took too long, jobs that weren't done properly, things like that. In the past, Francis would have been on top of those things, but now it all seemed too much for him.

It was a time for reflection in my life. When you reach your seventies, you want to have a sort of reconciliation with the characters in your story. I suddenly found myself wanting to see Peter Morley again. I wanted to have one last talk with him. I never loved the man, but he was the father of my son, and I wanted to tell him that. It was not to cast guilt upon him, but simply to set the record straight. He'd gone along all these years thinking that he'd had a casual night of frolic with me, and there was nothing that resulted from it. I wanted him to know that there was a baby born, that a soul came into this world, and it was partly his. I didn't expect much, but maybe he'd say a prayer once in awhile for his son, the way I did.

I got caught up in my life and forgot about Peter for a while. Then one day I was reading the newspaper and I saw his obituary. It listed his name as James Francis, the name he'd called himself since he left Rose. A wave of sadness came over me, and I regretted that I had never had that meeting with him.

I realized it was time to make amends with Rose. I didn't know how to track her down, but then she appeared, out of the blue.

I was in the John Wanamaker department store when I saw her. She was working as a saleslady in the Ladies' Dress Department. She was older, of course, but still tall and whippet thin, with a straight back and a clear eye. Her hair was white, and cut in a sensible bob, but otherwise it was the same Rose I knew so many years ago. I walked right over and presented myself to her.

"Why, I can hardly believe my own eyes. Is it Rose Sullivan I'm looking at?" I said.

Rose stared at me, and I was glad I was dressed in my fox trimmed gray coat, with my pearls at my neck, and my beautiful black wide-brimmed hat on. I was conscious of her running her eyes up and down me, but the light of recognition never dawned in them.

"You don't recall me?" I said. "Why, I suppose that's to be expected. It's been near 50 years since we last spoke. It's me, Mary Driscoll herself. Do you not remember that name, Rose?"

Then I could see shock and recognition in her eyes.

"Is it you, Mary?" she said. "This is a surprise, after so many years. To be sure, I am sorry I did not recognize you."

"Well, I doubt you've been thinking much of poor old Mary Driscoll all these years," I said. "I admit I look different, though. I've come up in the world, as you can see." I took one step back so she could get the full view of me.

Rose cast a skeptical eye my way. "Aye, you always wanted fine things, as I remember," she said. "I'm glad it has all worked out for you."

"Yes, it has," I said. "And what of you, Rose? How are things with you?" I could tell by looking at her that money was scarce in her life. She was wearing a plain gray dress, with a smidgen of makeup on her face, and a dot of lipstick on her lips.

"Oh, fine, to be sure," Rose said, impatiently, as if she knew I was judging her. "I am surviving, Mary. Now, can I help you? I take it you are here to buy a dress."

"Rose, don't be so formal," I said, grasping her by the hand. "We grew up together in Skibbereen, remember? I know there was a falling out between us, but it's late in life and we should forget those old grievances. Let's not hold on to those grudges the way so many of our countrymen like to do."

143

"I am holding no grudge," Rose said stiffly, taking her hand back. "It is only that this is my place of employment, Mary. I cannot be standing around chatting with the clientele about times past, you see. I am lucky enough to have a job in these hard years, and I want to keep it."

"I understand, Rose," I said. "But I believe it's a good sign that I happened upon you today. 'Tis a miracle, me running into you like this, and I don't want to pass it by. Let's go out to lunch, Rose, just you and I. We can talk over old times, and catch up on our lives."

"Out to lunch?" Rose said, raising her eyebrows at me. "After all these years, Mary?"

"Why not?" I said. "It's ten minutes before noon. You do get a lunch break, don't you? I know a lovely little tea room just around the corner on Market Street, and we could have a delicious lunch and a chat. What do you say?"

Rose seemed to soften a bit, and she said, "I'll have to ask Mrs. Hedges, my superior, if it's all right. I only get 30 minutes, though, so we can't be long. Wait here."

She left and went over to a gray-haired woman sitting at a desk, and said a few words to her. The woman, who I took to be Mrs. Hedges, took off her glasses and looked at me sourly for a moment, then spoke to Rose.

Rose came back and said, "We can go. But I must be back on time."

I took Rose to the Logan Tea Room, around the corner from the store. It was a place I liked, full of grand women like me in their elegant clothes and jewelry. I ordered finger sandwiches and tea for us, folded my hands, and said: "So, Rose, how have the years been for you?"

Rose sighed, as if it was a chore for her to speak of her life. She probably did not like recounting all the sorry details of how Peter Morley had left her.

"I would suppose you've heard a bit about me, Mary Driscoll," she said.

"No, I have not," I lied. "It may surprise you, but Philadelphia is a big enough place that a person can disappear from sight. You don't keep in touch with anyone I know. Of course, we travel in different circles now." It was a flaunting of my status, and I regretted saying it as soon as the words came out of my mouth.

I tried to make up for it. "I can understand why you might feel shy about telling me anything," I said. "I know I was the cause of some trouble for you when I wrote that letter to your father so many years ago, telling him you were about to have a baby out of wedlock. Sorry I am for it now, Rose. I was just a broth of a girl, you understand, and I was angry at you for making me lose my position with the Lancasters."

She narrowed her eyes. "You stole from Mrs. Lancaster, Mary."

"That I did, and it was wrong," I admitted. "I made a mistake or two in my youth, I am ashamed to say. You'll get no argument from me about the right or wrong of it. It's just, I wanted something better than what we had in Ireland, Rose, and I didn't know how to get it. And when I lost my position, well, it was like a death sentence. No proper lady would hire me after that, and I thought I'd

145

have to go back to the old country and live in shame for the rest of my life. Can you see how it would make me a bit mad?"

Rose said nothing, just sipping her tea and looking at me.

I reached across and put my hand on hers. "There's no use in digging up old grievances. Let the past be dead and buried, I say. I've come a long way since then, as you can see."

"You look well, Mary," she said, without smiling.

I appreciated the compliment, even though I knew she gave it grudgingly. "It's just a bit o' luck, I suppose. I had a hard time of it those first few years, Rose. I don't want to talk about all the things I did to keep body and soul together. I found myself living a desperate life, with a hard crowd of people.

"To be honest, Rose," I continued, "I often wondered what was going to happen to me, where I'd fetch up. After ten years of living hand to mouth, with some days not enough food to keep a field mouse alive, God smiled on me and I found a respectable position. I was hired at the seminary, of all places, to be a housekeeper for the priests who taught there! I got a nice, clean room, three square meals a day, and all the confessions my soul could handle."

Finally she smiled, and her eyes twinkled. "I never knew you to be a religious woman, Mary. I well remember how you wouldn't get out of bed on Sunday mornings to go to Mass with me."

"Oh, I was a pagan in those days, Rose, to be sure," I said. "I couldn't be bothered with priests and all their fussing. A few years of hardship will change a woman's mind, though. Another year and

I'd have surely become a nun, if they'd have taken me." I winked, and Rose smiled.

"A nun!" Rose said. "I have a hard time seeing you in a nun's habit. You always liked fine clothes, Mary."

"Lucky for me it didn't happen," I said, shaking my head. "I was saved by the priests, and I showed them my thanks by being the best cook they ever had at St. Charles Borromeo Seminary. It was a happy time for me, and I made a lot of good friends among the clergy. And all the good that's happened to me since is a result of my time at the seminary."

"You don't mean to say you're still working there, Mary?"

"No, Rose, I left that position years ago. I met a good Catholic man named Francis Dillon, a man who had a small bricklaying company. He was hired to work on one of the buildings at the seminary. I met him, and it was love at first sight. Oh, I don't say he lit all the candles for me, you understand, the way some others did. Francis was a quiet, simple man, but I had had enough of the other type, and I was ready for a man like him. And he has taken good care of me, I must admit." I emphasized the point by holding out my hand to show Rose the several gold rings on my fingers, including a glittering diamond wedding ring.

"I take it he's a man of wealth," Rose said.

"Not when I met him," I said, chuckling. "No, he was a simple bricklayer, with a half a dozen fellows working for him. But I have helped him to expand his business, so to speak. Why, today his company is one of the largest in the city for brickwork. He does all the work for the archdiocese."

"Does he now?" Her eyes widened in astonishment.

"Yes," I said, lowering my voice conspiratorially. "It so happens that one of the young priests I met back in my seminary days was Dennis Joseph Dougherty. You've heard of him, of course? The Cardinal?"

"I've heard of him," Rose said. "They call him 'The Great Builder' because he's put up so many new churches and schools."

"To be sure," I said. "And my Francis' company is usually the one doing the brickwork. The Cardinal has been good to us. Why, I can't tell you how many dinners I've been to at his residence, grand affairs with many important people at them. He's a very powerful man, you know. The Mayor, the Governor, all the politicians come calling on him. They want the Catholic vote. And there's me, Mary Driscoll from Skibbereen, talking to them like I was born to it. Can you imagine?"

I admit, I was laying it on a bit thick. I couldn't resist the temptation to gloat. I wanted to show Rose how far I'd come since our days back in Skibbereen. It was small of me, I suppose, but I've never claimed to be a saint.

"You've done very well for yourself, Mary," Rose said, in an overly formal manner. "I am happy for you."

"And how about you, Rose?" I asked. "How have things been for you? Are you still married to that handsome coachman named Peter?" Of course I knew she wasn't, but I couldn't resist.

I saw her flinch, and for an instant there was true hurt in her eyes. I should have asked God's forgiveness that I had spoken with such malice.

"No," Rose said. "He left me a long time ago, and he passed from this life two years ago last July. I have made my way without him for many a year now. I had three sons with him, but only one has survived. I am remarried."

"I am sorry to hear of your hardship," I said. "The handsome boyos cause us so much trouble don't they? It must have been the devil of a time for you, with three sons and no husband. Did you get the divorce papers? You say you are remarried. How do you stand with the Church?"

Now I was steering the conversation into troubled waters, and I should have stopped, but I couldn't.

A flash of anger came across Rose's face, and I knew I'd hurt her again.

"There was no divorce, Mary, if that's what you're asking. I had three small boys and no money when he left me, and I had no time to be thinking of anything but trying to survive. And I'll thank you for not judging me. I know it's not easy for you to do, since you're a pillar of the Church these days." She spat those last words out and folded her hands across her chest, her eyes blazing with anger.

I should have stopped, but again I blundered on. "But Rose, you are in a predicament. You can't receive the Eucharist--"

"I don't need any lessons in church law, Mary," Rose snapped. "I have done what I thought best. I haven't set foot in a Catholic Church in many a year, for just such a reason as that look on your face. I got that very look from priests and people in the pews, and I got sick to death of it."

"Then you don't go to church anymore, Rose Sullivan? What would your dear father think?"

Again, the wounded look in her eyes. "I don't care what my dear father would think. I go to a church where I'm accepted for who I am. It's my husband's church, and it's Episcopal. I'm married to Martin Lancaster. Do you remember him?"

Of course Aloysius had told me she'd married Martin, but some devilment in me kept me playing this charade, and I acted shocked.

"You don't mean to say the Martin Lancaster. . . the one who was a boy when we worked for the family. . . I always knew he had a soft spot for you, Rose, but you're not saying. . .?"

"Yes, I am saying," Rose said, glaring at me. "He has been a kind and gentle friend to me for many years, and now he is my husband. And I have never been happier, Mary. And now, if you will excuse me, it's time that I get back to work." She grabbed her purse, pulled a five-dollar bill out, slapped it on the table, and said, "I won't be needing any change," and walked out, with me staring after her open-mouthed.

When Rose left I sat there dumbfounded at what I'd done. It had been more than 40 years since I last saw her, and yet all the old anger and bitterness had boiled up inside me like a resentful spirit, and it made me want to hurt her. I had thought it was all gone, dead and buried, but it had risen up out of the grave. Why? Why had I tried to hurt her with my words? I should have been a happy woman. I had a loving husband, I had money, I had everything a woman could want.

Almost. It dawned on me that Rose had a son, Paul, and she was very proud of him. You could only look in her eyes when she spoke of him to see the love she felt. And she had grandchildren, another wonderful thing.

And me? Nothing. There was my son Luke, but I gave him away so many years ago, and who knew if he was alive still? He might have died years ago. And if he was still alive? He did not know the truth about his mother, of that I was sure. The people who raised him would not have told him the story of his birth.

Luke's story was like a hard knot of sadness inside me, always there at the bottom of every happy time in my life.

I knew at that moment I wanted to find my boy.

CHAPTER TWENTY

I had to know if my son was alive. If he was, I wanted to tell him the truth, that I was his mother. I didn't care that he would be angry with me -- why, I expected it. I just wanted to have a talk with him and let him know the truth.

I decided I'd go home and tell Francis of my plan. I'd never told him about my little boy, but now I wanted to make a clean breast of it. I knew he'd understand, and help me in whatever way he could.

But first, I wanted to stay in town and go shopping, because it always made me feel better. I loved looking at the latest fashions from Paris in the great stores in the city. It was a tonic for me, to be reminded that I could dress that way now. Inside me was still the girl who looked at the grand ladies in their dresses and wondered if she'd ever walk down the avenue in fine clothes like they did. I spent the rest of the afternoon going from store to store, and when I had my driver Dooley McCourt take me home, I had many packages to carry with me.

It was near dinner time when we finally arrived at the house, and again I took pleasure in the big house with its beautiful trees and bushes, its wide driveway and lush green lawn. You're a lucky woman, Mary Driscoll, I said to myself. You've come a long way from Skibbereen.

There was only one thing left to make it all complete, and that was to find my son.

I noticed that Francis' car was parked in the garage. He must have come home early today, as he had taken to doing lately. He was older now, and the long days on the job were tiring. He often came home a few hours early and took a nap before dinner.

I went inside with my packages, and I left them on a sofa in the parlor, then took off my hat and gloves, hung my coat in the closet underneath the staircase, and went upstairs. I was humming an old tune from my girlhood as I went up the stairs to check on Francis.

I found him lying in our bed with his back turned to me.

I touched his arm, and it was cold.

He was gone.

I turned Francis onto his back and put my face in his shock of gray hair, and I tried to fix his smell in my mind forever. It was a smell of brick dust and talcum powder, and the rosewater he used to try to get the smell of the construction sites off him. I reached down and took his hand, and I rubbed my fingers on the calloused surface of his fingers, still rough even though he hadn't lifted a trowel or carried a hod full of bricks in years.

"You were a good man, Francis Dillon," I said. "Too good for the likes of me. Too soon you've left me, my love. You never heard that word, 'love', from my lips, but love you I did. I should have told you so many times, Francis, but it's too late now."

I looked at the clock on the bureau across the room, and it said 6:00. I went over to the window and opened it and felt the evening breeze on my face. I gazed at the sky, dark already in the west, with the orange glow of the setting sun to the east. I could hear the rumble of trucks on the street and the whistle of trains in the distance. People were coming home from their work day, back to

153

their houses and rooms, back to their families and loved ones. Some had worries and sadness, some had joy, but every one was filled with thoughts of tonight and tomorrow, and next week, and next year. That priest, Father Boone, was right that people never look at what's right in front of them. They're always looking forward or behind, to a better time, and I was no different. I'd lived my life always thinking of what was coming next, of trying to get away from my childhood, and I'd missed the chance to just appreciate what I had with Francis Dillon.

A shooting star streaked across the western sky, and was gone in an eye blink. It made me think of the time I spent with Francis -- gone in an instant.

"I am sorry, Francis," I said. "So very sorry."

Why had I been so blind to this good man? He was the best man I'd ever met. Most of their lot had been shiftless, lazy dogs, too quick to make excuses for themselves. I learned not to trust them, to make my way in a world that was run by the likes of them. I fell into a way of thinking that made me blind to the good man right next to me. He had not a dishonest bone in his body, and he wanted only the best for me. I wasn't used to any man treating me that way, and I couldn't accept it.

And now he was gone, just like that. I supposed it was a heart attack. He had complained sometimes of chest pain, but I couldn't get him to go to a doctor or hospital.

"Hospitals are where you go if you want to die," he always said.

So now I was alone again. What was I to do, a woman in her 60s? And with all the country going to ruin, if you could believe the newspapers. They talked of the Crash as if it were the end of the world. I was glad I'd never bought stock, glad that I kept my money in a safe deposit box. I'll go and get it out tomorrow, I said to myself. When the bank opens I'll get my money out. We had a big safe in our office, and I decided I'd keep the money there, until things quieted down.

Money. It made people crazy, for sure. I knew I had to keep a steady hand on the business now that Francis was gone. Those laboring men who worked for Francis would not take kindly to a woman telling them what to do. I'd have to take control fast, or the company would go out of business, especially in times like this.

I went downstairs to the phone in the kitchen and called Joseph Flaherty, the local undertaker. I held back my tears while I told him about Francis, and he said he'd be right over.

When he came he expressed his condolences, and we spoke about the arrangements. It was over in no time, and Flaherty and his assistant took the body out to their hearse.

When Dooley McCourt came by in the morning, I told him to take me to the office, and to tell all the men to meet me there. They crowded into the room, all fifty or so of them, their faces sunburned and their hands calloused, each one with questions in his eyes, for they'd never had the experience of seeing me at the head of a room, speaking to them.

"I want all of your attention, now," I said, calling them to order. "Last night Francis Dillon passed from this good Earth, and sorry I am, for he was the best man I've ever met."

They all shook their heads and murmured their condolences to me, most of them looking at the floor in confusion and speechless grief. I gave them a moment, then held my hands out for quiet.

"I intend to have him buried at the cathedral," I said. "With all the good work we've done for this diocese, I expect them to clear their calendar and bury my Francis with pomp and ceremony. When I know the date I will tell you, and you will have the day off. We will do no work that day, in respect for Francis. I hope you will come to the funeral Mass, for it is only fair. He was a good man to work for, and I believe in your hearts you know that."

They muttered their approval, and I went on. "Now, as for the future of this company, I want you to know that I have no intention of selling it or closing down shop. Francis built this place with a lot of sweat and hard work, and I will not see it disappear like dew on the grass. I will keep it going, and I want to make it bigger and better."

More murmuring, and looks of confusion. I saw a few chins jutting out, and I knew what that was about.

"I see this doesn't sit well with a few of you," I said, putting my hands on my hips and glaring at them. "And well I know what the reason is. You don't think a woman can run this business, do you? This is man's work, and a man should run the show, is that right?" I looked around, and although most of them wouldn't meet my gaze, a few glared back at me with defiant looks.

"Well, it's a free country, and you're entitled to your opinion," I continued. "But here's what we're going to do: any man who doesn't think he can work for a woman, you're free to leave now. I don't care who you are, you can collect your pay and you'll have my good wishes, but you must leave right now. I'll not have

156

you work one minute for me if it doesn't suit you. Now, who wants to leave? Do it now, and be done with it."

There was more murmuring, and shuffling of feet, and then a big red-faced Irishman, a master bricklayer named McConnell, shook his head and said, "It's not right, and I won't do it. I've never worked for a woman before, and I won't do it now."

"Then you'll go with my good wishes," I said. "But begone now."

He scowled and walked through the crowd, then out the door, slamming it behind him.

I knew McConnell was respected, and I was afraid someone else would follow him out the door, but nobody did. Perhaps they'd gotten a taste of fear from all this talk about the stock market crash, and they didn't want to give up their paying jobs.

"Anyone else?" I said.

I gave them a moment to think about it, but no one moved.

"Good," I said. "Now, let us talk about the future of this company. Francis Dillon was a good man, but he was a bit too kind-hearted to manage a business like this. I know that some of you don't put your all into your work, and you're not above stopping in to a taproom during the day to have a nip, or even bringing a flask on the job with you. You may think I don't know who you are, but I've seen enough problems with shoddy work on jobs, and I know it's the same people on those crews over and over. I've asked around, and I have a good idea who's to blame. It's going to stop as of now, or you'll be on the street before the week is out. I'm holding all the crew leaders responsible, so if I find out anyone's been drinking on the job, his boss will be sacked as well."

I saw some faces redden, and the muttering started again. I knew what they were saying: There was nothing wrong with a man having a little refreshment on the job.

"So, you think I'm asking too much, do you?" I said. "Well, so be it. I'm in charge now, and we'll run this operation different. We've lost bids to other bricklaying companies in this city, just because the word has started to get out that Dillon's outfit produces shoddy work. We've lost a bit of our shine with the people in the Cardinal's office who make the money decisions, and I'll not have that situation go on. And let me warn you now: I see a bad time coming for the working man in this country, and there may be hard decisions that have to be made about this company for it to survive. I am not afraid to make those decisions, and when I do I will think carefully about who did his job the right way and who didn't."

I paused and looked each man in the eye. "Are there any questions?" I asked. There was still some muttering, but most of them shook their heads no. "Good," I said. "Now get out out there and show some pride in your work. Do a good day's work and let's turn this ship around."

The men filed out, and I turned to Dooley McCourt and said, "Now, drive me downtown to the Cardinal's office. I need to have a word with some people there."

Dooley drove me down to the gray stone building on 12th street, and I went up the marble staircase to the 5th floor, where the Cardinal's offices were. I walked down a long tiled hallway past secretaries typing away busily, most of them men, and then I went through the carved oak doors to the Cardinal's suite of offices.

158

I was greeted by a young priest, barely out of the seminary, sitting at a desk right inside the door. He had wavy blonde hair and spectacles, and he looked the soul of efficiency.

"May I help you?" he said.

"I'm here to see the Cardinal," I said.

"He's in a meeting and can't be disturbed," the priest informed me.

"I think he'll see me," I said. "I'm an old friend. Can you tell him Mary Driscoll is here?"

"I'm sorry, I told you he's in a meeting."

"Who's he meeting with, young man? I'm sure it can't be that important that he couldn't see me for five minutes."

"It's an extremely important meeting, with members of the building committee. I told you he can't--"

"The building committee!" I said, and strode right past him to the Cardinal's door. "Why, that's the very thing I've come to talk to him about. I see it's more important than ever that I have a word with him."

"Stop!" the young man said, scurrying after me.

He was too late, though, for I'm a fast walker when I want to be, and I pushed the door open and strode into the Cardinal's office before the boy could stop me.

Dennis Cardinal Dougherty was sitting at his big mahogany desk with the light shining on him from nearby windows, giving the

159

effect of a halo around his large head. He had several newspapers spread out on the desk, and a priest and a man in a three piece suit were sitting on the other side of him.

He did not look happy to be disturbed. The Cardinal had the build of a laboring man, with a stocky body and a square jaw. He looked like he could carry a load of bricks as easy as preside over a High Mass.

"I thought I told you that I was not to be disturbed, Father Quincy," he snapped to the priest who'd tried to stop me.

"I know, your Eminence," Father Quincy said. "But this woman just barged past me and forced her way in here."

"Begging your pardon, your Eminence," I said. "But it's me, Mary Driscoll, and I'll only take a moment of your time. I have a matter of importance to discuss."

Recognition dawned on his face, and he smiled, but only briefly. "It's nice to see you, Mary, but I can't meet with you right now. I'm discussing some important matters myself."

"Yes, young Father Quincy told me you were meeting about the building program," I said. "That's exactly what I've come to discuss. I think what I have to say will be of interest to you. I'll only need a moment, your Eminence."

The Cardinal sighed and drummed his fingers on the desk impatiently. "All right, I'll give you five minutes, Mary," he said. "There are things happening in the news that we need to discuss, matters of great importance." He dismissed Father Quincy with a wave of his hand, and the young priest went out and closed the door behind him.

160

"Sit down, Mary," the Cardinal said, motioning to an empty chair near his desk.

The other men stood up as I went over and sat myself down, then they took their seats.

"This is Bishop Mason," he said, pointing to a thin-lipped, gray-haired priest wearing the red sash of a Bishop. "And this is James Burton," he said, pointing to the beefy man in the three-piece suit. Both of them nodded in my direction, obviously not pleased to have this interruption to their meeting.

"Hello," I said to them, smiling politely. Then I turned to the Cardinal, and pointed to the newspapers. "I see you're reading the news about the stock market. It's not a pleasant story, is it?"

"Yes I have been reading the news," the Cardinal said, frowning. "We are a Church that focuses on eternity, but we also have to live in this world, and it's a world that runs on money. Any financial changes in the world affect us, and we have to take them into account. But, I digress. What is it that's on your mind that's so important, Mary?"

"Well, the first thing is, my husband Francis died last night," I said.

He raised his eyebrows. "Francis Dillon? I saw him only last week, at the site of the new school we're building, St. Jerome's. He looked as healthy as a horse. Is it true, Mary?"

"It's true, sorry though I am to say that," I said. "My Francis died in his sleep last night."

The Cardinal reached across the desk and put his hand on mine. "I am truly sorry. Have you made arrangements for his funeral?"

"That is a matter I wanted to discuss with you," I said. "I would like him buried from the Cathedral."

"Here?" the Cardinal said, his eyes widening. "Why, Mary, I don't know if it can be done on such short notice. I'll have to check the calendar."

I gripped his hand hard enough to make him wince. "You do that, Dinny. I know I'm not one of the high and mighty you cater to in this town, but Francis and I have served you well over the years, helping you to build all those schools. We made our contributions to the church, also, as you know. You could always count on us to give when you needed it."

He pulled his hand away, and rubbed it with his other one. "I will see what I can do, Mary. Talk to Father Quincy on your way out. Tell him to meet with me after I'm finished here. I'm sure we can schedule a funeral Mass for later in the week."

Then he put his hands down on the desk, and pushed his chair back as if he were going to get up and walk me to the door. "I'll see you out," he said. "I am so sorry for the loss of Francis. He was a good man. Now, if you'll bow your head, I'll give you a blessing."

"No thank you, your Eminence," I said. "For I'm not finished yet. I have another matter to discuss."

He seemed to lose his patience then. "Really, Mary, I can't give you any more time. I have important business here."

162

"And that's the very subject I want to speak to you about," I said. I pointed to the newspaper. "The news is not good today, and I have a feeling it's only going to get worse. Times are about to take a bad turn, your Eminence."

The man in the suit cleared his throat and objected. "I don't know what you're talking about," he said. "It's a temporary downturn in the market, that's all. Things will be better by the end of the week, I am certain."

"And I am certain they will not," I said.

His faced reddened and he shifted in his seat. "Really, I don't know where you get off, making statements like that, Madam. I am president of the second largest bank in Philadelphia, and I have my finger on the pulse of the economic life in this city. I don't think that a woman has the knowledge--"

"You may bluster and tut tut all you want," I said. "But if you're such an expert, did you see this coming? Did you advise the Cardinal to sell any of the stock the Church owns, so they wouldn't lose money when this happened?"

His face turned a purplish red, and his lips moved, but it took several seconds before any sound came out. He turned to the Cardinal and protested. "Your Eminence, I don't know who this woman is, but I will not have my financial acumen questioned by her."

The Cardinal folded his arms across his chest. "She's right, Mr. Burton. It's obvious to me you didn't see this coming. We could have used some of your financial acumen weeks ago, before our portfolio lost half its value. Let her speak."

"Good," I said. "I know I'm not an educated woman, but I have a good head on my shoulders, and I study people, especially men. I've been watching men all my life, Cardinal, and I know how they think. They're herd animals, you see, only they all think they're not. They want to believe they're independent, but they're always looking around to see what the next fellow does, and then they copy him. The last few years they've all been on a mad quest to get rich, because they've heard 'tips' and 'inside information' that have convinced them there's money to be made in the stock market. Each one of them thinks he's the only one who's got the inside track, and so all of them, all the way down to shoeshine boys and street sweepers, has been investing every penny he has, trying to make a big payday."

"That's ridiculous," Burton said. "I've never heard such--"

The Cardinal held up his hand. "Let her continue," he said.

"The other thing about men is they scare easily," I said. "Men don't like to admit it, but it's true. Fear spreads like a virus among them, and it's spreading now. Once the panic started and the stock fell, fear took over. I can see it in the eyes of every man out there on the street. They're scared, more scared than they've been in a long time. That's what is driving this, and it will cause more devilment before it runs its course. You're going to be getting less money in the collection basket, Dinny. And you should probably scale back the building program."

He frowned. "This is not what I want to hear," he said. "But somehow I fear you're right, Mary. There were times in the last few years when I thought things were getting out of hand. God does not give us too much happiness on this Earth. The good times had to end sometime, as they always do."

"And that they will," I said. "So, I've a proposal to make. I predict you'll be trimming your sails for a few years, your Eminence, cutting back on all the building programs. I've got almost three score men who need to make a living to support themselves, and I want to take care of them. I'm going to trim some of the deadwood, but most of them are good men, and I want to do right by them. All I'm asking is for your consideration, that you keep me in mind for any jobs in this diocese. I don't care if it's sweeping out the churches, or cleaning leaves out of the rain gutters, I'll find you men who can do it. If there's no brickwork to be done, my men will do just about anything else you can think of, for whatever you can pay them. They're good workers, and you'll not be disappointed with them -- the ones I keep on my payroll, anyway."

He folded his hands into a steeple in front of his face. "I will see what can be done, Mary. I have a big job to do here, and I can't focus only on your company. I'll see what I can do."

"That's good enough for me," I said, standing up. "And now I'll take that blessing."

He winced. "I'll give it to you, but I must say you're a hard-headed woman, Mary Driscoll. I don't think many women would have come down here and talked to me like that on the day of their husband's death."

"Francis was a good man, God bless him," I said. "But he's gone, and I must carry on. I'll take your blessing, but I must also take matters into my own hands if I want to eat my next meal. It's always been my philosophy, Eminence, and it's served me well."

"Let's hope it still does, Mary," he said, chuckling. "Let's hope it still does."

CHAPTER TWENTY-ONE

Things went downhill when the 1930s arrived, to be sure. The news got worse and worse, and it was a struggle for me to keep the business running. I had to give the men a lot of jobs they'd never done before, and some of them grumbled about it.

I often spoke to Francis at night, alone in my bed, and asked his advice. He didn't answer me much, but then he was always a man of few words. There were times, though, when I could see him smiling at me, and he'd say, "Just do your best, Mary. That'll be enough."

I wondered if it was, though. I hated to let any of the men go, knowing how hard it would be for them to find employment, and I scraped and scrambled to get any kind of work possible. I cut our prices, I made myself a regular visitor to the Cardinal's office, and I let it be known that Driscolls' wasn't above doing charity work, just to keep the men busy. I still had some friends among the rich and mighty in the city, but many of them were suffering, and they weren't inclined to throw any work my way.

Throughout it all I managed to keep slipping my envelope of money in Father Boone's door once a month, and I felt good about that. His parish had been hard hit, and when Dooley McCourt took me through that neighborhood, I saw the lines outside the soup kitchen the good father had set up. I stopped in the church once or twice, and I noticed the people in the pews had a desperate look about them, as if they were praying for their next meal.

The years started to wear on me. I was a woman in my 70s now, and I could feel more aches and pains in my body. I'd soak my tired feet in a bath every night, and it was hard to keep my energy up.

I couldn't show any sign of weakness in front of the men, though, especially not when I got a visit from some men in suits with wide lapels and wide-brimmed hats, who came to see me one Friday afternoon.

"My name is Mister Arguello," a skinny man with a five o'clock shadow said, sitting down across from my desk. "And this is Mr. Pistone," he continued, pointing to a bulky man in a pinstriped suit that was too tight for him. The big man sat down also, although he looked like an elephant trying to fit into a child's chair.

"What do you want?" I said. They had interrupted me when I was doing some work in the ledger book, and I was in a bad mood, because of all the red ink I was using.

"We visited your husband a few years ago," Arguello said. "I haven't been back here for many years, but it looks like you're surviving these terrible times we're having. I'm surprised."

"Why, did you think the company would go under when my husband died?" I said.

He frowned. "No, it's just that I thought--"

"You thought a woman couldn't run this company, I know," I said. I sighed. "Mr. Arguello, it's late on a Friday afternoon and I'm tired. Could you get to the point, so we can finish up here?"

He looked offended that I had talked to him in such a blunt manner, but he brushed some lint off his lapel and then got down to business.

167

"We want to have a business arrangement with you," he said.

"What sort of arrangement?"

"Well, we would protect this fine company, basically, make sure that nothing bad happens to you or your men out there. It's a scary world, Mrs. Driscoll, and we wouldn't want anything to happen to you. We'd charge a small monthly fee for this service, of course."

"I see," I said. "I'm imagining this is the same proposal you made to my husband ten years ago. Is that right?"

"Why, yes," he said. "Actually, it was an associate of mine who made the proposal. Unfortunately, something came along that prevented us from following through."

I chuckled. "Yes, and his name was Aloysius O'Toole, wasn't it? He threw a monkey wrench into your plans. Aloysius was good at that type of thing."

His face darkened. "He drove a hard bargain with us. But, as you know, he's gone now. It's taken a few years for things to settle out, but now we feel it's the right time to negotiate with you again."

"Negotiate?" I said, laughing. "Is that what you call it? I'd use a different word."

"You can use any word you want," he said, his dark eyes flashing. "The truth is, you're going to pay us for protection, lady, and that's it."

"Protection from what?"

He smiled. "From people like Mr. Pistone."

Just then the big man got up and went over to the wall, where there was a large wedding portrait of Francis and me. It was behind glass in a gilt-edged frame. The big ox took it off the wall and then in one motion he smashed it against a desk, shattering the glass to pieces. He threw the remains of it on the floor and stomped on it, breaking the frame. Then he took the picture out and tore it to shreds. I gasped as if from a blow to the stomach.

"It's a terrible shame," Arguello said, shaking his head. "Mr. Pistone gets angry sometimes. And he does violent things when he's angry. I wouldn't want that to happen again. Do you see the value in our business arrangement now?"

I reached in the bottom drawer of my desk and pulled out a gun that I knew Francis had kept there. I took it out calmly and pointed it at his chest.

"Walk out of here now," I said. "Or you'll be carried out. It's your choice."

A grin spread across his face. "You wouldn't do it. You're a woman, and women--"

I pulled the trigger and shot him in the shoulder. I was only a few feet away from him, so it was hard to miss. His eyes widened in shock, then he reached for his shoulder and started cursing me in Italian.

The big man looked shocked also, and I pointed the gun at him and said, "Get your friend out of here right now, you big lunk, or I'll put a hole in you too. Get out, and if I see either of you come in here again, I'll aim better next time."

The big man rushed over and helped his friend to his feet, and ushered him out the door. On the way out Mr. Arguello finally got command of his English, and he shouted, "You made a big mistake, lady. You'll pay for this!"

Then they were gone, and the door slammed behind them.

My secretary Theresa Logan came rushing in, red-faced and flustered.

"What happened? Are you all right? Who were those men? Did you shoot them?" She was talking so fast she was out of breath and had to sit down across from me.

"Calm yourself," I said. "It's nothing special. Those two goons tried to threaten me, and I shot one of them. That's the end of it."

"But Mrs. Dillon," she said. "That man is hurt. He'll go to the police."

"Men like that never go to the police," I said. "No, he'll find a way to get that wound taken care of, and the police won't know a thing about it."

"But will they come back? Oh, my, I think I'll be afraid to work here now."

I looked at her sternly. "Theresa Logan, I'm surprised at you. You should know by now that giving in to fear is exactly what men like that want from us. They'll have us working for them in no time, if you have that attitude. If it's too much for you, dear, then I suggest you leave now. I'm not going to live in fear of the likes of them, and

I don't care if they do come back -- I'll have more of the same for them."

I was putting up a good front, but I admit my legs were shaking so much I didn't know if I'd be able to stand up. But for a woman to run a brickwork company in that time, I had to show no fear at all.

So I went about my business as if I didn't care. Before long, word spread among the men that I'd faced down a couple of toughs, and they looked at me with new respect. I had no problem with them treating me like a weak widow anymore.

I lived with the thought that Arguello and his friend would come back some day, and although I wouldn't let it faze me, I began to think about tidying up my affairs. I was a woman in my 70s now, and even if the gangsters didn't get me, I was faced with the same fate everyone on this Earth has.

It was time to find my son.

CHAPTER TWENTY-TWO

Not long after that I ran into Martin Lancaster at City Hall. I was there on some legal business for Dillon Brickwork and I noticed a familiar face among all the lawyers, police, politicians, clerks and prisoners roaming the halls. I saw an old man with kind blue eyes in a rumpled suit, talking with some shady looking character on a bench in the waiting room of an office. I knew instantly it was Martin, even though I hadn't seen him in years. I remembered Rose telling me she was married to Martin now, and that he was a criminal lawyer who specialized in defending small time crooks, people on the edges of the underworld. I thought a man like that might know how to find my son.

I waited, and when Martin stood up and ushered his client through the door, I went over to him.

"Hello, Martin," I said. "Do you remember me?"

He peered at me, and I could tell he did not.

"It's Mary Driscoll," I said. "I used to work for your parents. Rose Sullivan and I worked at your house in Chestnut Hill, when we were only just girls."

A light dawned in his eyes and he reached out and clasped my arm. "Mary Driscoll! Why of course! It's good to see you after so many years. How are you?"

"I'm as good as can be expected for a woman my age," I said. "But I have an old woman's feet, and I'd like to sit down somewhere and have a chat. Is there anywhere we can go?"

172

"Of course," he said. "I am embarrassed to say I don't have a fancy office. My clients are not always able to pay my fees, so it's difficult finding the money for rent. I use various offices loaned to me by my attorney friends when I need to meet with a client. At times I meet in restaurants, too. There's a nice little cafe down the street where I sometimes go. Would you like to go there and get some coffee?"

"I would like it very much," I said.

He took me to a little hole in the wall restaurant a couple of blocks away, and we sat down at a greasy table and ordered coffee.

I got down to business right away. "I understand you defend criminals. Is that right?"

He smiled. "Yes, that's right. I have taken a different path than the one my father assumed I would take. If I had gone that route I'd have a plush office in some established Philadelphia firm now, I'd have an estate on the Main Line and breed horses on the side." He laughed. "I've never really liked horses. I suppose it was that incident from my childhood that traumatized me."

"I remember," I said. "When the horse ran away with our carriage. I thought we'd all die, for sure. You were very frightened, as I recall."

"Yes," he said. "It made a great impression on me. So, I suppose it's best that I'm not rich enough to be in the horsey set on the Main Line."

"Am I right in thinking that you deal with, let's call it the seedier side of life?" I said. "That you know your way around the underside of the city?"

He sipped his coffee, then smiled. "I deal with all sorts of clients, it's true. No matter what they've done, however, they are entitled to legal representation under our system of law. I am happy to provide that. Why do you ask?"

"Because I need help in finding someone," I said. "Someone I haven't seen in many years. Someone who may not even be alive anymore. I can't give you a description of what he looks like, or even his name. I have barely anything I can tell you, but I'm still desperate to find this man. I don't know where to turn with a quest like this, and I thought maybe a man like you could be of some help."

"That's a tall order," he said. "And I'm not really in the missing persons business. However, as you said, I know some private investigators who may be able to help. Who are you looking for?"

"My son," I said.

Martin's eyes widened, and he sat back in his chair. "You have a son, but you don't know where he is? Did he get in some kind of trouble?"

"Not that I know of," I said. "It's a long story, Martin. You may remember that your mother dismissed me from her household when she accused me of stealing."

"I do remember that," Martin said, wincing. "It saddened me, Mary. I was always fond of you, and I couldn't believe you'd done something like that."

"Well, I'm ashamed to say I did do it," I admitted. "I was just a foolish girl from County Cork, Martin, and I made a mistake. I wanted fine things for myself, and I thought I'd get them by taking a few of your mother's jewels. I didn't think she'd notice. Anyway, Rose found the jewels and she reported me to your mother. I carried a grudge against her for years because of that -- I wanted her to keep her mouth shut instead of doing what she did -- but I'm past that now. I made the mistake, and I can't blame Rose for it."

"We all make mistakes, Mary," Martin said. "Especially when we're young."

"Yes, and we have to pay for them," I said. "And I did pay, for quite a few years. I couldn't get another job as a serving girl, for no one would hire me with that blot on my record. So, I scuffled around and did some things I'm not proud of, just to keep body and soul together. I was angry about my fate, and the bitterness festered inside me. It was during this time that I ran into Peter Morley, Rose's husband. You remember him?"

Martin's face clouded. "Yes I do. He worked for my family also, as you recall. And when Rose married him I was very sad. I didn't think he was good for Rose at all, and as it turned out, he wasn't. He left her with three small children. He also, I found out later, had relations with my sister while he was still married to Rose. He caused Rose a lot of pain."

"Aye, and me also," I said. "For he was the father of my child."

His eyes widened and he put his coffee cup down with a clatter. "Are you serious, Mary? That man certainly caused a lot of pain and confusion in this world."

"Indeed he did," I said. "He was trouble, that fellow, and I should have stayed away from him. But I knew he was Rose's husband, and I'm ashamed to say I wanted to hurt her, in any way I could. I happened to run into him, and one thing led to another. I was playing with fire, and I got burned. It was only one night of passion, but when I found out I was expecting a child, I decided not to tell Peter Morley. I just went off by myself and had the baby, at a house in New Jersey, and then I gave it away."

"I know that happens," Martin said, shaking his head sadly. "It's something women do when they feel they don't have a way out. I hate to see it happen, but I've helped a few women in that situation over the years."

"I got to see the baby only once," I said, "and he was a healthy boy with big brown eyes. He smiled at me, and they took him away. I've thought about him every day for the rest of my life, Martin. I'm getting on in years now, and I'd like to find out if he's alive. It's an old woman's foolishness, I suppose, but I'd like to see his face one time before I die."

Martin looked at me with compassion in his eyes. "I'll try my best, Mary, but there's not much to go on. Do you know the name of the place where you had the baby?"

"It was called Serenity Farm," I said. "I remember the name above the gate in front of the place."

He wrote it down on a piece of paper. "And what was the date?"

"I could never forget that," I said. "It was June 16, 1902."

He wrote that down also. "That would make him a man of 33, then."

"Yes," I said. "And a right handsome one he'd be, I think, judging from what he looked like as a baby."

"Spoken like a true mother," Martin said, smiling. Then he turned serious. "I'll do what I can, but I can't promise anything. I have an investigator who is very smart and capable, and knows more about tracking people down than the police. I have to be honest, though. Even if he finds your son, this person might not want to see you. He might be very angry about what you did. Or, he might not know anything about it. His new family might never have told him."

"I understand," I said, "and I will accept whatever happens. I just cannot stand not knowing anymore. I must know what happened to him before I leave this world."

"Then I'll see what I can do," Martin said. He stood up and said, "I have to be back in court in a little while, so I must be going. It was good to see you, Mary. Shall I tell Rose we met?"

I smiled. "Of course! I wouldn't tell her about the business with Peter, though. I know it was long ago, but it might wound her anyway. I would not want to hurt her now."

"Don't worry," he said. "I won't tell her."

We walked back to City Hall, and I shook Martin's hand before he went into the building. "I wish you much happiness with Rose," I said. "And I hope you both appreciate the love you have. It's a wonderful thing when love comes into your life. I had it for a long while with Francis Dillon, but I didn't appreciate it while it lasted. It's a gift, Martin."

"I know," he said. "And I'm thankful for every day with Rose. I hope we have many more years together."

That was the last I saw of him, for he died a week later.

It was Rose who told me he died. I had not heard from Martin in weeks, and then one day a letter arrived.

"Dearest Mary," it said. "I found your name and address in some of Martin's papers. Apparently he was handling a legal matter for you. I wanted to tell you that he died last month, in a tragic accident. You will have to find another attorney to handle your business. I have lost the man who meant most to me in the world. Rose."

I felt sadness for Rose, of course, but the loss of Martin meant that I had little hope of finding my son, and that, I am sorry to say, bothered me more. I should have reached out to Rose and comforted her, since I knew so well what she was going through, but it was like my own son had died along with Martin. I had no hope that anyone else could track down my boy. Sure, there were private investigators I could hire, but Martin had worked with the people who lived in Philadelphia's shadows for so many years, I thought he was the only person who could find his way through that world.

I wrote a letter to Rose and offered my condolences, but I put off seeing her. I could not bear to sit across from her and act as if my life was normal when it was not. I had no energy to go on.

It was a time when I needed to summon up my energy, though. My men told me there were suspicious looking characters loitering about our jobs, and some tools had been stolen. I knew it was a sign the gangsters were trying to scare me, but I couldn't bring myself to do anything about it. Dooley McCourt kept telling me to go to the police, but I said no. Then one night someone threw a rock through my front window, and after that Dooley moved in to protect me. I was numb to it all, showing neither anger nor fear about what was happening.

But then one evening the doorbell rang at my house and there was a man in a dark brown raincoat and a wide-brimmed hat, carrying a briefcase, standing on the porch. He told me his name was Mr. Jennings, and he was a private investigator hired by Martin.

CHAPTER TWENTY-THREE

"I have some information that might be useful," he said. "May I come in?"

I invited him in to the sitting room and sat him down across from me on the sofa. Dooley hovered close by in the kitchen, making himself busy cleaning up the supper dishes and creating lots of noise so Mr. Jennings knew he was there.

Mr. Jennings opened his briefcase and pulled out a plain manila envelope. "Mr. Lancaster asked me to find someone for you," he said. "He died, as you know, but I wanted to finish the assignment. I take my work very seriously, Mrs. Dillon. It took some time, but I believe I found the person you were looking for."

He handed me the envelope, and I held it for a moment, trying to calm myself. I was trembling as though from bitter cold, and I had to take deep breaths to calm down.

"You will find it all in there," he said. "I ran into a number of dead ends, but then I went to the Salvation Army. They have an office that helps to reunite mothers with children they gave away. With their assistance, I was able to find some records, and I followed the trail further. Once I had the name of the family he was given to, I tracked them down. His adoptive father is still alive, and I interviewed him, and found out where your son is living."

"I don't know if I can open this envelope, Mr. Jennings," I said. "My heart is beating too fast."

"Take your time, Mrs. Dillon," he said, without smiling. "But I think you will be interested in the contents. I think you will want to open it, when you are ready." He stood up. "I will be going now, Mrs. Dillon. I hope what I found is satisfactory to you."

"What do I owe you for your trouble?" I asked.

He paused, and said, "Nothing. Take my fee and give it to. . . well, you'll understand when you open the envelope."

He left, and I sat for a long time holding the envelope. Dooley Mc Court came in the room and said, "Who was that fellow?"

"A private investigator," I said. "He tracked down someone from my past. It's all here in this envelope."

"Why don't you open it?" he asked.

"I'm finding it difficult to do," I answered.

"Would you like me to do it?"

"No, no. I will open it in good time. I just need some more time, that's all."

"Well, I'll be in the next room, if you need me," he said.

He left, and I picked up the envelope. All those years of wondering, of yearning, of praying to know if my son was still alive, and now I was going to get an answer. My heart was pounding in my chest, and my hands were shaking.

Open it Mary -- this is the answer you've been waiting for.

I turned the envelope over and ripped it open. Inside were a set of official documents, some mimeographed copies of records,

181

and some letters on official stationery. With trembling hands I paged through them, my eyes not able to focus at first, but then a name jumped out at me.

Lorcan Boone.

Father Lorcan Boone, according to another document, from the archdiocese of Philadelphia, certifying that one Lorcan Boone made his priestly vows in 1922, at the Cathedral Basilica of Sts. Peter and Paul in the city.

It couldn't be. I looked through the papers in a state of shock, my mind denying the evidence of my eyes, trying to find a reason not to believe what I was looking at.

But it was all there. The baby, known only as Boy 2, because he was the second boy born that day at Serenity Farm in Medford, New Jersey, was adopted by a family named Boone who lived on Philadelphia's Main Line. He was named Lorcan and baptized in the Episcopal Church. He went to the local public school until he was 17. Somewhere along the line he must have converted to the Catholic faith, for when he was 17 he entered St. Charles Borromeo Seminary.

There was a list of his parish assignments, and it ended with Sacred Heart of Jesus, the same parish I had been sending money to for the last ten years.

I dropped the papers to the floor, then fainted.

Dooley McCourt revived me with a wet cloth, and when I finally came to my senses I realized what I had to do. I wanted to see my son, to tell him who I was, to give him the truth.

I well knew that he might not believe me, so that is why I determined to write everything down, as plainly as I could. I would write the story of my life, holding back nothing, giving all the details as best as I could remember them, and that way my son would at least have the facts. If he chose to ignore them, or deny them, or hold a grudge against me, that was his business. Indeed, I would not have been surprised had he thrown me out of his presence, for the story I had to tell might wound him desperately. I could understand if he wanted to lash out at me, though he may be a godly man who did not want to let anger rule his heart. I could only hope for his forgiveness, and some small portion of understanding from him.

I went to work with pen and paper, and it took me two weeks of constant writing to get it all down. I cried many times during the writing of it, though there was some laughter too. I had a sense that time was running out, because my men said there were many suspicious characters hanging around the jobs, and even some scuffles here and there. My men were stout-hearted, and they wouldn't be scared off, but Dooley McCourt said he could tell they were worried.

When I finally wrote the last page I put my pen down and said a prayer.

God, please let my son look at these words with compassion and understanding. I made the decisions I thought were right. I know I did wrong sometimes, but I tried to do good also. Let my son judge me on the whole of my life, not one day out of a lifetime.

It was evening, and I put the story in a manila envelope and told Dooley McCourt to get the car.

"Where are we going?" he said.

183

"To Sacred Heart of Jesus church," I said.

He looked alarmed. "It's nine o'clock at night," he said. "What do you want with going to a church at this time?"

"I want to visit the pastor, Father Boone," I answered. "I have something to deliver to him."

"Can't it wait till tomorrow?" he said. "I don't like going in that neighborhood at night."

"No," I said, putting on my coat and hat. "It cannot wait another minute. Now, get the car, please, and make it quick."

He shrugged and said, "Okay, Mary, as you wish."

Dooley drove me down to Sacred Heart of Jesus, through the neighborhood of narrow streets where the houses were so close to the curb you could see the families gathered around the radio in their living rooms, listening to their favorite shows. The streets were nearly empty, and I saw the steeple of the church looming above the houses like a great black finger pointed at the sky. There was a light on inside the church, because the stained glass windows were glowing from within.

"Pull over here," I said to Dooley, and he found a parking spot across the street from the church. I got out of the car expecting to go inside and say a prayer before the Blessed Mother altar and then ring the doorbell at the rectory next door and give my package to the housekeeper.

But to my surprise I saw Father Boone come out of the church and close the big wooden door behind him, pull out a set of keys, and lock the door. I started across the street, and I called to him.

"Father! Father Boone!"

He turned in the direction of my voice, and just before I got to the curb, I felt what seemed like a heavy blow to my back, knocking me forward and making me drop the envelope with my story in it, and I saw the papers scatter across the asphalt. I tried to get up, but I was hit with another blow, and then I heard a sound like a car backfiring, although I realized at once what it was. I had been shot. A second later I heard the sound of tires squealing and a car speeding down the street, and Dooley was running over to me, panic in his voice.

"Mary!" he shouted. "For God's sake, are you all right?"

I looked up to see the eyes of Father Boone above me.

"My God, is it Mary Driscoll?" he said. "What's happened here? Have you been shot?"

"Yes I have," I said. I could feel the warm blood leaking out my back, and my life energy leaking with it.

"Let me get you to a hospital," Dooley shouted. "Father, can you help me?"

"No," I said. "It's too late. I'm sure of that. Can I have the Last Rites, Father? Please."

"Of course," he said. "But I'm sure you'll be fine, Mary. There's a hospital two blocks away. We'll get you there and--"

"No," I said. "There's no use of that. But I want you to have the story. The papers. Pick them up, Dooley, and give them to the priest." I turned to Father Boone. "It concerns you, Father. Please read it, and forgive me if you can."

"Of course I will forgive you," he said. "And God will too. Your sins are forgiven." He took out his crucifix, blessed himself, and started to say some prayers in Latin.

"Thank you my son," I say.

I see his eyes widen at the word "son".

You'll get an answer to your question, Luke, in due time.

* * *

Now, I can see the stream moving on, rushing on its way past tree and hill, making little eddies in the center and along the banks, here and there catching on a tree branch or a rock that interrupts its flow. But it always finds a path around the obstacles, and continues ever onward on its way.

What a strange, terrible, and wonderful journey it has been.

Still flowing.

THE END

THE END OF BOOK SEVEN

This is the last book in the Rose Of Skibbereen series. Look for the other books on Amazon at amazon.com/author/johnmcdonnell.

A word from John McDonnell:

I have been a writer all my life, but after many years of doing other types of writing I'm finally returning to my first love, which is fiction. I write in the horror, sci-fi, romance, humor and fantasy genres, and I have published 24 books on Amazon. I also write plays, and I have a YouTube channel where I post some of them. I live near Philadelphia, Pennsylvania with my wife and four children, and I am a happy man.

My books on Amazon: amazon.com/author/johnmcdonnell.

My YouTube channel:

https://www.youtube.com/user/McDonnellWrite/videos?view_as=subscriber

Look me up on Facebook at:

https://www.facebook.com/JohnMcDonnellsWriting/.

Did you like this book? Did you enjoy the characters? Do you have any advice you'd like to give me? I love getting feedback on my books. Send me an email at mcdonnellwrite@gmail.com.

Printed in Great Britain
by Amazon

25317996R00108